I0522536

The only way I could go on living without Tracey in the present was to find her in the past...

She was wearing beige dress pants, a gold belt, and a white blouse, with a little makeup and red lipstick, enough to accent her natural beauty without overwhelming it.

She stepped in front of me, eying the roses my limp fingers dangled in front of her. "Hi," she said, and then she took the roses from me. I watched her sniff one of them in the hallway.

Then Tracey's mother arrived downstairs.

When I looked at Tracey's mother in the hallway, I had my first glimpse of Tracey as a woman. Their features were nearly identical, most notably the doe eyes and silky blonde hair.

If I could've photographed Tracey, as she looked in her forties, alongside her mother that night, anyone who saw that picture, who didn't know them, would've thought that they were sisters.

The same pattern would develop between Tracey and her daughters.

Is there someone who lingers in your memory—someone who makes you wish you could revisit your past, knowing what you know now?

At forty-two, Ryan Tremblay still fantasizes about Tracey Simpson, a girl he fell in love with in high school but never spoke to. When Ryan returns to his hometown after his father's death, he's haunted by visions of Tracey. Then he opens his old high school yearbook one night and stares into her face until he drifts off to sleep. When Ryan awakens the following morning, it's June 7, 1991, and he's eighteen again. Thus begins an obsessive journey that transcends distance, madness, and time.

KUDOS for The Yearbook

In *The Yearbook* by David Grove, Ryan Tremblay is a forty-two-year-old man who is still obsessed with Tracey, a girl he went to high school with. He goes back to his hometown, after his father dies, and travels back in time through his old high school yearbook. Now he's eighteen again, and can relive the past, this time making it come out like he wants, or can he? The author puts forth some interesting ideas in this cute, clever, and thought-provoking tale. A very intriguing read. *~ Taylor Jones, Reviewer*

The Yearbook by David Grove is the story of a man obsessed with his past. Our hero, Ryan Tremblay, is still in love with his high school crush, Tracey Simpson, a girl he loved from afar, never spoke to, and can't get over. When Ryan is forty-two, his father dies, and Ryan returns to his hometown. Up in his old bedroom, Ryan stares at his old yearbook from 1991, his senior in high school. When he wakes in the morning, he's eighteen again, his mother and father are both still alive, and it's June 1991, for the second time in his life. Now he has a chance to change the past and have a relationship with Tracey. But reliving the past isn't as easy as Ryan might have thought. *The Yearbook* is a poignant and charming story of one man's quest to change his life and his trip back in time, which doesn't quite turn out the way he'd hoped. An interesting and thoroughly entertaining read. *~ Regan Murphy, Reviewer*

ACKNOWLEDGMENTS

Thank you to Lauri at Black Opal Books for agreeing to publish this book. Thank you to Faith and Jack for helping to make this a reality.

The Yearbook

DAVID GROVE

A Black Opal Books Publication

GENRE: FANTASY/MYSTERY/ROMANCE/TIME TRAVEL

This is a work of fiction. Names, places, characters and incidents are either the product of the author's imagination or are used fictitiously, and any resemblance to any actual persons, living or dead, businesses, organizations, events or locales is entirely coincidental. All trademarks, service marks, registered trademarks, and registered service marks are the property of their respective owners and are used herein for identification purposes only. The publisher does not have any control over or assume any responsibility for author or third-party websites or their contents.

For Maureen

Chapter 1

Every September, I thought about the start of a school year, mostly the first semester of my senior year of high school, when Tracey Simpson sat beside me in our English Literature class. On September 28, 2015, I was forty-two and still obsessed with Tracey, the great love of my life.

That was a gray, mournful day, in more ways than one. I spent most of the morning behind a standing desk, staring at a picture of a high school graduating class. I'd isolated the girl in the orange dress who'd reminded me of Tracey.

The girl had doe eyes and silky blonde hair in the picture, which I took in June 2014, and I was instantly mesmerized by her bright, gushing smile. At first glance, she looked just like Tracey.

Her name was Laura Hartley. She entered the University of British Columbia in the fall of 2014.

Tracey and I had graduated from Port Moody Senior Secondary in June 1991.

I was still behind the desk when a man and a woman, a couple, tentatively entered my small studio.

I opened my photography business in 2010, the year I finally moved out of my parents' house, the year after my mother died. The studio was located in Langley, a densely populated municipality in Metro Vancouver. I described myself as an adaptable, affordable, friendly photographer who specialized in budget weddings.

The couple stood just inside the doorway. "My brother got a new camera," the man whispered, repeating the line I'd heard so many times before. "He'll take the pictures."

"I want a professional photographer," the chubby woman snapped. "Your brother's an idiot."

"We're broke," he said matter-of-factly.

Besides the picture, I had the book *Lewis Carroll: A Biography* with me. I alternated between reading the book and staring at the picture, looking down, pretending not to be listening.

I was getting ready to pounce when I turned on my phone, which had been lying dormant on the desk. I saw a series of frantic messages, sent in rapid succession, all from Bradley Tremblay.

I hadn't spoken to my older brother in over two years.

"Ryan!" Brad said. "I've been trying to reach you all morning."

"What do you want?" I demanded, eying the couple.

"It's Dad," he said. "He had a heart attack."

My relationship with my father was defined, in the preceding months, by terse calls and messages, and I couldn't, at that moment, recall the last warm exchange between us. He was extremely disappointed in me.

The phone clung to my fingers, but I couldn't feel it. I was looking out the window, recording the colors and shapes, when I heard my brother clear his throat before he continued. "He's gone," Brad intoned. "He's dead, Ryan. Dad's dead."

&&

Early the following morning, after breakfast, I packed a suitcase and then returned to my hometown, Port Moody, British Columbia, after a long absence.

I entered Port Moody through the Barnet Highway, which only had one traffic light from beginning to end. With the North Shore Mountain Range and the sparking blue waters of the Burrard Inlet on my left, the drive was smooth and weightless.

As I neared the end of the Barnet, my eyes expertly deciphered Port Moody's crescent shape. Then the four-way intersection appeared in front of me, which was the moment when I felt myself crossing over.

When my car came to a stop in front of the intersection,

I looked straight ahead, past the opposite light, down Albert Street, where Port Moody Senior Secondary was tucked away. The school was surrounded by a forest of green trees.

My eyes followed the straight road, which had a gradual upward incline, to the top of the hill, where the range of my view ended, in front of the entrance to the school's upper parking lot. When I looked diagonally to my right, I could just barely see the outline of my high school through the trees.

I made a right turn onto Snake Hill and began the steep climb. I ignored the right turn that appeared halfway up the hill and climbed to the top, which was the highest point in Port Moody.

When I reached the three-way intersection at the top of the hill, my car was alongside the parking lot of the defunct K Y Market, the store my friends and I visited daily during my Banting Junior High years.

I made a right turn onto the long, winding road that separated College Park, the residential neighborhood I grew up in, from the rest of Port Moody and the world.

I drove past Glenayre, the residential area in which I'd attended pre-kindergarten, and the Fire Hall, where two hulking firefighter/paramedics were dispatched from one fateful morning in March 2000, seconds after I'd called nine-one-one and said, "I think my mother's had a heart attack or a stroke."

I stopped at the invisible College Park border, looked

to my left, and saw Westhill Park, a grass playfield inhabited by a baseball diamond and a soccer pitch, surrounded by a jogging path and a thick forest with many trails.

They'd added a row of fitness machines to the playground area since I'd moved away, and the lacrosse box I used to play ball hockey in had been given an extreme makeover. It'd been converted into a multi-sport facility to accommodate the needs of the growing population.

The seasonal outdoor swimming pool was empty.

❧❧❧

I was thirty-seven years old when I felt able to live outside of 333 Princeton Avenue and take care of myself. This was only made possible because of the sizable legacy I took from my mother's death.

I could count on my two hands the number of times I'd visited College Park and the house since I'd moved out. I hadn't been inside my old bedroom since December, at Christmastime, which meant that nine months had gone by since I'd looked at a picture of Tracey.

At the front door, I found a plump garbage bag, which was full of leaves. The bag was untied, begging to be closed with one of Dad's strong double knots.

The furnace roared from the basement as soon as I walked through the front door. After I took off my jacket and shoes, I stood still in the hallway and gravely stared ahead into the dim living room, which hadn't changed much since November 17, 2009, the day Mom died.

The portable bed she had slept on, not in, remained in place alongside the sliding glass door, stripped, except for the pillows. The commode and the wheelchair were down in the basement with the twenty-one storage boxes that contained all of her belongings.

If I hadn't been home when Mom had her stroke, her death would now be nearing its twentieth anniversary instead of its tenth. I wasn't sure if I'd done the right thing.

She had the stroke in the master bedroom. I was sitting in the computer room down the hall, hiding from her, when I heard her body thud against the floor.

It was a concentrated, heavy thud and sounded as if her body had compacted itself into a ninety-seven pound medicine ball that fell straight down, dropped from a high place.

I immediately ran down the hall. I was surprised, but not at all shocked, when I saw Mom lying face down on the floor, between the front of the bed and the doorway, her pantyhose on her calves.

I waited downstairs after I called nine-one-one, barefoot and in my pajamas. I stood, unwashed, just outside the front door and looked up and down the hill in front of the house, waiting for an ambulance that turned out to be a multi-purpose fire truck.

I stood on my toes in a futile attempt to match the eye level of the firefighter/paramedics, both of whom were wearing thick-soled shoes, which they did not need to tower over me. They pushed past me into the house and raced upstairs.

We—the paramedics and I—saved Mom's life that morning but not the mother I'd known before the stroke, who died sometime between the morning of the stroke and the subsequent brain surgery.

After Mom returned home from the hospital, in a wheelchair, I looked after her until Dad retired in 2005. I didn't want to think of myself as a caregiver, but that's what I was. I got her up in the morning, emptied her bedpan, dressed her, gave her breakfast, changed her diaper, put her on the toilet.

I was afraid to leave the house and College Park in case she needed me.

The stroke left Mom paralyzed on her left side, and she rarely left the living room between 2000 and 2009. Dad tried taking her upstairs to bed with him one night, which did not go well, with the bedpan and everything else, and the portable wasn't big enough for two. My parents never slept in the same bed again.

The only times Mom left the living room, and College Park, were for doctor's appointments, the platelet count checks, and bingo and bocce at the Dogwood Pavilion, the social recreation center Mom visited once a month.

No one visited Mom, who had always boasted about her many long-standing friendships and how well liked she was. They stayed away in droves. "I've got so many friends," she would say when she was mad at me, "and you've got nobody."

"Where the hell are they?" I'd yell back at her.

Although the doctors told us there was no reason why she couldn't regain full use of her left side and even walk again, there was no improvement. She fought Dad and me every time we tried to stretch her left arm and mobilize the shoulder blade. Sometimes she pulled my hair and scratched my face. She stopped eating.

I could still smell the incontinence odor eliminator spray, the Shiseido revitalizing emulsion she applied to her crumbling face, the wetted-through bed pads.

I brought my head down on the bed, over the spot where my mother's chest would've been at night. After she had her eight o'clock pills, before I went upstairs to bed, I'd always listen for her heartbeat.

The clicker was on the glass table. It was Mom's security blanket. She sank into her chair every morning after breakfast and explored daytime television, which was a new world for Mom, whose busy schedule had kept her away from the house every morning and afternoon before the stroke. She loved *The Price is Right*, and she became addicted to *The Young and the Restless*, which shocked me, recalling how Mom had always belittled daytime soaps and expressed sorrow for the lonely, pathetic people who watched them.

She watched *Jeopardy* and *Wheel of Fortune* before the stroke, back to back, every night, and this continued, though she couldn't see or hear the television very well from the bed. I just wanted her to sleep.

Dad had a clear view of the bed and Mom's empty chair from his chair. It was a devastating sight after she died, sobering with both of them gone.

Mom's urn sat on the right edge of the mantel. I grabbed it and shook her.

The furnace was still blasting away when I stepped into the basement, past the laundry room, and faced the sliding glass door.

When I entered the furnace closet, I felt the force of the heat on my back and neck. I reached down to the cold cement floor and went through my old papers, from cardboard boxes that were packed at the end of high school. I found a pile of three-ring binders, mostly from grades eleven and twelve, underneath the boxes. The binders were all full. Every sheet of lined paper was covered with my illegible, ugly handwriting.

I also found board games, textbooks from Douglas College and Simon Fraser University that their bookstores were unwilling to buy back from me, and two dusty old photo albums. The oldest one was filled with pictures of my parents from the early years of their marriage, along with the only pictures I'd ever seen of my paternal grandparents. We were a small family.

The second photo album contained childhood pictures of my brother and me. The album began with baby pictures, then moved to baseball and soccer team pictures, and then to our class pictures from Seaview Elementary. I saw the entire cast of supporting characters from my childhood, between kindergarten and the seventh grade.

The rest of this album was devoted to pictures of three boys who became fast friends in the first grade and were clearly inseparable at one time. Most of those pictures were taken at the house, inside and outside, mostly in the basement.

As I looked at myself in those pictures, I listened for the sounds of my long-lost friends, whom I hadn't spoken to in nearly twenty years.

I went upstairs to my room. Before I entered my old bedroom, I stood in the middle of the upstairs hallway and stared into the darkened bathroom. I listened to the annoying, steady drip of the leaky shower faucet. The master bedroom door was on my left. It'd been left ajar.

I listened for Dad's cadence but not for long. I turned and faced the two other bedrooms in the hall. I reached for the knob on my door. I was thinking about the yearbooks and seeing Tracey Simpson again.

I dropped my suitcase on the floor and flopped onto my bed. Then I stared at the three dressers in the bedroom, which were pushed together and extended across the front of the bed, sitting between the edge of the closet, which was on my left, and the window. The single dresser, which was closest to the closet, contained a cluster of socks and underwear in the top drawer.

Four short comic book storage boxes rested on the four-drawer double dresser, which sat directly in front of the bed. Those boxes contained the remains of my once glorious collection, which I assembled over the course of my lifetime and dismantled in a matter of hours. All that was left were the unsalable dregs, the degraded, unwanted books that would never increase in value, no matter how long I lived.

The bookcase stood in the top right corner of the bedroom, against the wall, on top of the third dresser, which jutted out, away from the others, toward the window. This dresser only had one drawer. This was the yearbook drawer.

I turned away from it and slid over to the window, where I had the clearest view of the whole of Port Moody. The Burrard Inlet sat squarely in the center of this three-dimensional picture, beneath the opposite end of Port Moody, Port Moody's northern edge, to the left of downtown Port Moody. The traffic between the Barnet Highway and downtown Port Moody sounded like a continuous breeze.

Whenever that window was open, the sounds played tricks on me. I heard a pounding noise, which played every day after I returned home in 2015. It sounded like it was nearby but originated way out near Port Moody's eastern border, where construction workers were nailing wooden boards onto metal stakes for the rapid transit line that was going to run through and underneath Port Moody.

I'd stood in front of the window countless times before, staring into the Inlet's waters, which were black, unable to conjure up a scenario in which I would ever be near Tracey again. Once again, I felt the dull ache in the roof of my mouth and the sting behind my eyes that heralded tears.

Then I sat down on the front right corner of the bed, inches away from the yearbook drawer. The yearbooks were hidden underneath a pile of crayon drawings from Seaview Elementary. The yearbooks were stacked in chronological order, from 1987 to 1991.

I peeled away the Banting Junior High yearbooks and grabbed the Port Moody Senior Secondary yearbooks from 1990 and 1991. Then I slid across the bed with them until I was sitting upright while leaning back against the headboard.

I reached for the 1990 yearbook first. My left thumb bent the spine with little effort. I opened it and tried to shake the sticky, yellowing pages back to life.

I stumbled over my grade eleven headshot and forced myself to look at it, at myself, for only the second or third time in my life. I quickly turned the page and flipped through the rest of the yearbook

I paused when I saw a picture of myself sitting in the school cafeteria with Michael Gillies and Stuart Malley, my former best friends, the only friends I'd ever had.

Then I turned to Tracey Simpson's headshot. Her glowing forehead, sparkling doe eyes, and wide smile gleamed through the fingerprints and shadows.

I put down the 1990 yearbook and opened the 1991 yearbook, which was nearly worn out. I stared at Tracey's senior headshot, and then I flipped over to a color picture of Tracey. In this picture, she was sitting in front of a row of lockers, alongside Robin Daly and Shannon McKenzie, who were Tracey's only real friends at Port Moody Senior Secondary.

I pored over every word of Tracey's yearbook inscription, as I'd done so often throughout the nineties, wondering what and who was on her mind when she wrote it.

Cheers to the Class of 1991!
Tracey will remember those just passing through,
but a special few will remain forever golden.
Thanks to amazing parents for everything.
Gallant spirits can never be defeated.

I flipped back and forth between the two images, contrasting the black-and-white headshot with the color picture. I kept going, back and forth, over and over, until I could no longer see clearly.

I closed the 1991 yearbook and lay on the bed, looking up at the ceiling. Then I turned to my left to face the radio, which sat on the nightstand between the bed and doorway.

I opened the nightstand drawer. I couldn't see the over-sized picture amidst the junk as I reached inside. I blindly dug around until I felt the edge of the picture, which had gotten lodged underneath the drawer over the years. I removed the picture, carefully, knowing this was the class picture that was taken behind the school in June 1991.

I was surprised by how much color and sharpness the picture had retained after more than twenty-four years. It looked like it could have been taken in June 2015. Everyone in the picture looked so animated. I believed that Michael and Stuart were with me again. I could feel their arms around me and hear their voices.

My eyes drifted across the picture and found Tracey. There was dead silence.

I held the picture against my chest.

Chapter 2

I was able to piece together Dad's dying moments by talking to the people who were near the house when Dad dropped dead: the landscaper working on a house across the street, and the UPS courier who drove past the house as Dad was running around like a headless chicken. They both told me they saw Dad drop a leaf blower then clutch his chest.

I walked out of the house in my wedding suit and looked down at the bag of leaves. I decided to let it sit until I had Dad's ashes. I found more leaves outside, thirty-three of them, which I scooped up with my fingers and dropped into the open bag.

I left College Park and returned to the three-way intersection at the top of Snake Hill. The K Y Market was on my left. If it had been a Saturday or Sunday, and I was seventeen or eighteen, I could've been on my way to the Petro-Canada station at Burquitlam Plaza with my friends. But the purpose of that trip was to oversee the burning of my father's remains.

When I drove past the Burquitlam Plaza, I looked to my left and saw that the strip mall had fallen into steep decline. Its veil of charm had been completely ripped away. The loyal, struggling retailers had been denied the right to death with dignity. The main entrances were clogged by lumbering, noisy machines.

There were two condominium towers under construction, and there was the transit station project that took away the Dairy Queen and my Petro-Canada.

The Burquitlam Funeral Home was located two blocks west of the plaza and was mentioned in every other obituary I'd seen in the *Tri-City News*, the twice-weekly community newspaper that served Port Moody. In no mood to shop around, Brad and I immediately agreed to send Dad's body there.

The funeral director stood behind me in the viewing room with a perfunctory look of concern on his face as he watched me approach the cremation casket. Pushing myself forward, I peered into the casket, at my father, Carl Tremblay, seventy-two years old.

He'd been neatly dressed. He looked so lustrous and rested that I was sure he was going to open his eyes and spring to life at any moment. "Come on, Dad," I mouthed, my shaking right hand touching his face. "He met Mom on a blind date," I mumbled, turning to face the funeral director, whom I caught peeking at his phone and yawning. "He was in advertising," I continued, pushing the words out like a shot putter driving the heavy metal ball. "He started his own ad agency, which was very successful. He was responsible for a lot of radio and television commercials that you might remember. He loved hockey and the Canucks. He was a season ticket holder and never missed a game. He once played a round of golf with Sean Connery."

I slid my fingers through the brown and silver hair that documented my father's life. This exposed the gray I felt responsible for.

ოჯოჯ

Dealing with Dad's death was, on some level, exhilarating, in terms of the flurry of activity it generated. But writing the obituary, unlocking and sorting my memories of him and then condensing my feelings into less than 200 words, left me emotionally spent.

Instead of submitting the obituary through the *Tri-City News*'s online self-serve system, I personally delivered the text, along with a picture of Dad, to the classified representative—a young woman who was clearly in her first job after college or university—I'd spoken to on the phone. I did anything I could think of to prolong the process, which enabled me to make believe that I still had a father.

"Do you think it's a good picture?" I asked her inside the cramped office. "I can find another one."

"It looks fine," she assured me, with a touch of exasperation in her voice. "The obituary will be in Friday's edition."

"That's only three days from now," I said.

∽∾∽

The following morning, after breakfast and cartoons, it took me exactly twelve minutes to walk from the house to Seaview. I lived farther away from the school than almost all of the rest of the kids at Seaview. Most of them lived either in the Evergreens or the Woodlands, the neighboring townhouse complexes that bordered the school. I could still go through every street, door to door, and point out where every kid lived.

I was five, and as alone and friendless as I was at forty-two, when Mom forced me out of the house one afternoon and took me down the hill to find some kids for me to play with. I met my first group of friends that day. They were all gathered behind one of the Woodlands buildings, including Michael and Stuart. Everyone was five. We entered Seaview together.

Several other kids lived in College Park, at various

depths, but no matter where we lived, our world was small. Everyone congregated within two blocks of the school. Until we were allowed to ride the buses by ourselves, which didn't happen for most of us until the fifth grade, there was nowhere else to go. There was nowhere to hide.

There was a memory of a childhood adventure attached to every blade of grass, sidewalk, and street. But when I stood at the edge of the school parking lot and looked around, nothing appeared.

The kids were all gone. Obviously, many of them lived in or near Vancouver and throughout British Columbia. The rest were spread out around the world. Regardless of where they'd moved to, their adult lives had taken them far out of my reach.

It was the most astonishing feeling in the world, depressing and frightening, standing alone in front of the school, knowing that I was the last one left.

Seaview was an age-segregated school when I was there, divided between the primary kids and the intermediates. When I was a primary, I was limited to the front of the school during recess and lunch hour, watched over by the kindhearted Ms. Turcotte, the redheaded primary monitor.

As primaries, my classmates and I played soccer and touch football on the lumpy, uneven lawn outside Mr. Stoffberg's classroom. We were still oblivious to the presence, the existence, of the girls, who hovered around us, spread out across the pavement.

Our world expanded dramatically when we entered the fifth grade and became intermediates. Besides being able to go anywhere, the intermediates were given free license to bully the primaries and were seated in the front rows during assemblies.

I walked through the parking lot and past the hopscotch squares, headed for the back of the school. I stopped in front of the gymnasium door then looked down at the thin line that separated the primaries and the intermediates. It was a perfectly straight white line, which ran from the door to the edge of the forest.

I heard children inside the gym, thumping up and down on the floor. The door had been left open. I looked inside and saw the kids playing dodge ball. Then I looked over at the stage on which the Nativity scene was reenacted every year at Christmastime. I was on that stage myself in grade seven, in front of the entire school, when I became spelling bee champion, the only award I received in school and throughout my life.

The gym floor was covered with tables for our graduation ceremony, which was held in June 1986. When I looked through the Port Moody yearbooks, I could find twenty-six people I went to Seaview with. I went to school with most of them for twelve years, not including kindergarten, but I had a feeling that most of them would barely remember me, which I thought was much worse than being completely forgotten.

Twelve years was a long time for us to get to know each other, which we certainly did. But there was all the difference in the world between familiarity and friendship, and I was a forty-two-year-old man with no friends and no one to talk to.

The area behind the school looked exactly as I'd remembered it, except that the tetherball posts on the pavement had been crudely dislodged from the sockets, leaving rusty stumps. I walked along the gravel field, which everything else behind the school revolved around. I moved past the playground, which was on my right, staring into the once beautiful, mystical forest, which had withered away.

The gravel field was perhaps forty yards wide. When we were all strewn over the field at recess and lunch hour, splintered into the groups that emerged toward the end of the fourth grade, it looked as if we were on different planets.

I kicked at the gravel, looking for bones, dust, any relics from when we were there. Then I walked up the hill to the dilapidated grass field above the school, where many of the organized baseball and soccer games were held in the early eighties. It had turned into a derelict wasteland. The carcass of the diamond and the mound were barely visible through the loose, soggy grass. It looked like hell.

The scope of the exodus was apparent to me when I looked down at the entire school, but it didn't register as strongly as it should have, given my age. I still honestly believed that we would all be together again, at the beginning, on the other side.

From the top of Seaview, I left the school through the trees, through the upper section of the Woodlands, heading for Glenayre and the K Y Market, on my way to Banting Junior High. I was on the sidewalk, facing away from the school and the Woodlands, when I heard the kids break for recess.

I stopped and listened to them run outside. Their combined laughter and motion blended into a wonderfully bizarre melody. A horde of skipping rocks striking the water's surface at the same time, I thought.

⋐⋑⋐⋑

I stopped in front of the K Y Market lot, facing the three-way intersection and Port Moody's southern border. When I crossed the street from the K Y Market, I headed south and entered Coquitlam, the city that bordered Port Moody on the east and south.

Instead of following the main sidewalk, I walked through the adjoining residential neighborhood, wanting to retrace the steps my friends and I took every morning when we attended Banting Junior High, between 1986 and 1989. I ended up standing in front of a chain-link fence, where I had a clear view of the entire school.

The grass field in front of the fence was followed by a

400-meter oval gravel track and then the school itself, which easily covered the full width of the field and track it towered over.

I dug my fingers into the fence, scanning the school, going through every inch of the place, left to right, top to bottom, every classroom and hallway. I remembered everything.

When I was a student at Banting Junior High, which was known as Banting Middle School in 2015, the school's nickname was the Banting Braves. This was represented, on the side of the school, by the painted image of a screaming Indian warrior with war paint on his cheeks.

When I walked past the Band room, I cringed at the memory of myself attempting to play the cumbersome bass clarinet during my three-year sentence there. Choosing Band in the first place was ill-advised—Drama was the only other option, which wasn't much of an option for me because of my stuttering—and my choice of instrument defied logic. While everyone else chose the clarinet, flute, saxophone, trombone, the trumpet, I decided to become the school's first bass clarinet.

My choice was even more baffling because it separated me from Michael and Stuart, who both played the trumpet. Because they were in the other class, with the brass instruments, the three of us were only together during the concerts and the Tuesday night practice sessions. I needed them.

Although I sat with the clarinets, behind the flute section, I knew I was very different.

Chapter 3

I waited until four to drive down the hill to Port Moody Senior Secondary, which had been renamed Port Moody Secondary School since I graduated. I was confident that most, if not all, of the students would be long gone and I could wander around undetected.

There were two other cars in the upper parking lot when I arrived at the top of the hill. I got out of my car and looked down at the school, probing its defenses.

The most noticeable outward difference, from when I was a student there, was the loss of the smoke pit and the adjoining walkway. The open space had been filled with a lobby.

The nearest entrance, the eastern one, was only a few steps away from the edge of the parking lot.

When I entered the school, I was immediately confronted by the entirety of the school's reconfiguration and renovation on the upstairs floor when I instinctively reached for the weight room door, which would've been directly on my right at Port Moody Senior Secondary. I found air.

I heard basketball sounds. I turned a corner and went through a side hallway, headed toward the gymnasium. When I stood outside the gymnasium, where I secretly watched the Port Moody Blues boys being put through intense drills, I was at the far end of the long hallway that ran past my locker in grade twelve. When I turned and looked toward the opposite end of the hall, I saw Tracey.

Her back was turned to me, and she had a binder and a textbook tucked under her right arm. She was taking measured, short, uniform steps down the hall. When she reached the end of the hall, she turned her head ever so slightly and looked through with me with icy detachment. Then she disappeared around the corner.

By the time I reached the end of the hall and turned the corner, she was gone.

I walked over to the other side of the upstairs floor, stopping between the library and the Math classroom. All of the lights were on in the library. When I looked inside, through the glass, and saw ahead of me the bookshelf that ran across the far wall, I relived the most disastrous scene from my life…

ᕳᗏᕲ

One afternoon in the last semester, late in the year, Tracey and I happened to be in the library at the same time, though I was completely unaware of this fact until it was too late. I was seated at one of the tables with Michael and Stuart, in front of the far wall, when I carelessly, foolishly invoked her name. "Tracey Simpson," I said to them. "She's in my Math class. Have you seen her?"

"She's in my Chemistry class," Stuart chortled, slowly turning his head toward the library's rear window wall. "She's a smart girl."

"Do you know anything about her?" I asked Stuart. "Do you know if she has a boyfriend?"

"There's only one way to find out," Stuart said, shuffling his chair away from the table.

I saw Tracey when Stuart rose from the table and looked over at the study carrels. I could see what he was going to do, and I wanted to leap from my chair and tackle him. But my entire body went limp.

"You don't ask, you never know," Michael chimed in.

I watched in stunned horror as Stuart calmly walked over to Tracey. She looked up at him impassively, and then he pointed in my direction and started talking to her. I covered my eyes until he returned to the table.

"I hate you," I said to him as he sat down.

"When were you going to make a move?" Michael asked me.

"Now she knows," Stuart said, patting the table.

"What did you tell her?" I asked him, lowering my head.

"I told her: 'My virgin friend is hot for you and wants to ask you out but is too scared to say anything.'"

⁕⁕⁕

I stood in front of the library door until the sound of a janitor working down the hall broke my trance.

I walked over to the Math classroom and stared through the glass. The first thing I noticed was a tablet computer on the teacher's desk, connected to a projector that was mounted onto the ceiling. When I turned my head and pressed my left cheek against the glass, I could see the front of the desk in the back right corner.

⁕⁕⁕

On Thursday morning, approximately seventy-two hours after the moment of Dad's death, I collected the cremation certificate and urn from the funeral home. I immediately returned to College Park.

My brother's car was in the driveway. I saw his face on the driver's side door. When I walked through the front door, I heard Brad's footsteps upstairs. As he walked downstairs, I pictured the agile, fearless knight I'd idolized growing up.

But the sight of his pot belly shattered the illusion into a million pieces.

Brad arrived downstairs with a full, weighty box in his arms. I held out the urn.

"Hey," he said, pointing at it. "Is that Dad?"

"Who else could it be?" I asked him.

"Wow," he said. "I can't believe it."

I kicked off my shoes and solemnly entered the living room, hoping my brother wouldn't follow me.

After I placed Dad's urn on the mantel alongside Mom's, I turned to look at Brad, who set the box down on Mom's chair and sighed. His face was puffy and red.

I looked inside the box. It was full of games and toys. The *Dungeons & Dragons* paraphernalia unleashed a flood of pleasant memories, all involving Brad, who was the best—the kindest and most unselfish—Dungeon Master an inexperienced and mentally-challenged fighter could have ever asked for.

"We can meet with the lawyer next week," Brad said. "Don't worry about the house. I'll take care of it. I've already typed up a listing. It's ready for the website."

"What are you talking about?"

"I'm going to sell the house," he said. "No commission. We're family."

"I don't want to sell," I said.

"In this market, I think we could get at least one-five, easy," he said.

I looked over the scorched earth where Mom and I suffered together after the stroke. "I took care of her after she had the stroke," I said, pointing at Mom's empty chair and the naked bed. "I was with her, in here, practically twenty-four hours a day."

"That's because Dad and I were working," Brad said. "We were going to bring in a nurse, remember? You said, 'no way.' You wanted the money. It was the best job you've ever had."

I shoved Brad hard, but he would've fallen to the floor with much less effort. "Bradley Tremblay," I said derisively. "Personal Real Estate Corporation."

He got up quicker than I expected. I thought he was going to say something else, but whatever he saw in me made him scurry out the front door.

∽∾∽∾

In my bedroom, I opened the 1991 yearbook again. I skipped over the headshots and Tracey and turned to the basketball team picture.

In the picture, I stood between Michael and Stuart on the bottom row. My hair was unkempt, and my large head was disproportionate to my skinny body. My small hands were holding a basketball as if it were a pumpkin. I walked unseen into the gym and approached my teenage self. I turned and looked at the camera and the photographer.

I was in bed when I closed the yearbook, just after I watched the photographer take the picture. I turned to my left and set the yearbook down on the nightstand.

Then I buried my head under the covers.

ℭ∞ℭ∞

I awoke under the covers. My fingers rubbed against silky smooth sheets. Sunlight poked through the blinds, illuminating my lanky arms.

I'd left the radio on. I caught the tail end of EMF's "Unbelievable," which was followed by Jesus Jones's "Right Here, Right Now" and then Clay St. Thomas and Janice Ungaro, Zed 95's original morning hosts. They were giving away advance screening passes to the film *Robin Hood: Prince of Thieves*.

I looked around my bedroom in fascination.

The yearbook was gone from the nightstand.

I heard Mom's authoritative footsteps climbing the stairs.

Chapter 4

During those dreary days in the living room after the stroke, I sometimes snapped and smacked Mom around the head, conscious of the stitches from the brain surgery but blinded by rage and stress.

I could deal with her incoherent babbling and the drooling, and even her wetting herself and the bed. But when she crapped herself before I could pull down her diaper and get her on the commode in time, I wanted to kill her.

"I feel sorry for you," she'd say to me whenever I hit her or called her names like animal or retard. "You're the one who's retarded. You're going to spend the rest of your life alone."

I was still very much ashamed of our unnatural union and the awful things I'd done and said to her when we were alone in the living room, when I heard the knock on my bedroom door. When the door opened, the image of a wraith in a diaper was replaced by an assertive, perky woman in her late forties.

Bernadette Tremblay, clad in a dark business suit, was carrying a laundry basket.

"Mom," I exclaimed, sitting up.

"I've got appointments and showings all day," she said, quickly hanging up my clothes. "I think we'll order pizza. Are you going out with the boys tonight?"

"What day is it?" I asked.

"It's your favorite day of the week," she said. "Hey, do you have your yearbook yet?"

I reached for her face, hands shaking. "Mom," I said, going blank.

"I love you," she said. She kissed me on my forehead and left cheek on her way out.

I crawled to the front of the bed and opened the yearbook drawer. The 1990 yearbook was on top. It was in much better shape than the last time I'd seen it. The junior high yearbooks were underneath. But my original copy of the 1991 yearbook was missing.

I heard the toilet flush downstairs. "Goodbye," Mom said.

I stood on the upstairs landing and listened to her walk out the front door then lock it behind her. She checked it twice before she walked away.

I ran into the master bedroom, keeping my head low until I reached the window. Then I inched up until I could see the diamond white pearl Lexus. I watched Mom get into the car and drive away.

I turned on the television in the living room and raced through the channels, pausing at Bryant Gumbel on *Today*, and *Live With Regis and Kathie Lee*, and MuchMusic, which was Canada's music video station. I was most interested in the local information channel, which had the date burned into the screen.

It was June 7, 1991.

I was watching baseball highlights when I heard a car pull up outside. I turned off the television and looked out into the hallway. As I walked out of the living room, I glanced over at the mantel on my way to the front door. When I reached the door, I slid my hand over the polished, warm wood, and then I waited for two oncoming sets of feet to land on the doorstep.

I opened the door and stared at Michael and Stuart.

They barged past me and rushed into the kitchen before I could say a word. I looked outside, past my blunt, functional Honda Civic. Once again, I worshipped Michael's muscle-bound, yellow 1987 Ford Mustang, with the black trim, the wedge shape, the sloping hood, and the sculpted roofline. What I'd missed the most was the hoarse, meaty rumble of the five-liter V8 engine.

After I closed the door, I stood between the hallway

and kitchen and watched Michael and Stuart raid the cupboards and fridge. I also saw their older faces.

As Michael, Stuart, and I were driving away from the house, I spotted Mom's face outside one of the houses on our block. It was splashed across a For Sale sign that had been spiked into the lawn.

My parents were among College Park's most important citizens. Dad was president of the College Park community association and the Port Moody Rugby Club. Mom chaired the neighborhood advisory committee and once ran for a Port Moody City Council seat, narrowly losing.

∽∾∾

After Mom died, we received condolence calls from Dr. Noble, our family doctor; the Dogwood Pavilion; and Sutter Realty, the real estate company Mom terrorized for many years.

After Dad's cremation, I received condolence calls from Dr. Noble's son, the rugby club, and there was a generic sympathy card from the owner of the advertising agency Dad founded.

∽∾∾

The most surreal aspect, for me, of experiencing June 7, 1991 a second time was how quickly I adjusted to, and moved beyond, the shock of seeing Mom again and reuniting with my friends. By the time I entered the backseat of Michael's car, I'd already gone far down the road toward accepting this as reality.

The rest of the morning, prior to my reunion with Tracey, unfolded predictably and reasonably in my mind, where the past and present had always been interchangeable. I really couldn't tell the difference.

After leaving College Park, Michael drove toward the three-way intersection in front of the K Y Market, the same route we took to the Petro-Can on the weekends. But instead of turning right and heading toward Burquitlam Plaza, we turned left and descended to the bottom of Snake Hill.

Michael and Stuart started off talking about basketball, and then they transitioned to what they'd watched on television the night before, and then they moved to girls and the prom. They were very predictable.

"Have you found a prom date yet?" Michael asked me.

"I've got someone in mind," I said.

Stuart turned and grinned at me. "Beggars can't be choosers."

"Here's Stu's best friend," I said, making a fist with my right hand then shaking it like was a martini.

When we reached the bottom of Snake Hill and made the right turn onto Albert Street, we were surrounded by teenagers. I couldn't find Tracey in the crowd, but I knew that I would see her in Math class.

The school day typically started at ten to nine, but there was no bell or buzzer to enforce this. It was understood.

When I looked at my watch, I realized that, after more than twenty-four years, I was less than thirty minutes away from seeing Tracey again.

Chapter 5

I found my locker combination in the school office, where everyone's digits were kept on file.

As I was staring inside my grade twelve locker, Becky Dodd, one of my Seaview colleagues, arrived at her locker, two doors to the right of me. She was one of the people I'd gone to school with for twelve years, part of the Seaview-Banting-Moody group. But she wouldn't give me the time of day.

I'd never forget the occupant of the locker on my right in grade twelve. When Darren Clayton arrived at his locker, all of my long-held fear bled out of me and left me with simmering anger.

I didn't know what I had done or said to Darren, who'd gone to Banting, to make him hate me so much, or why he'd became so obsessed with the proportionality, shape, and size of my head, which Darren nicknamed The Cranium.

Our fight, the only fight I had throughout my adolescence, took place during a ball hockey game in the gym, on a Friday night in May 1991, the only Friday I could recall from grades eleven and twelve when I wasn't with Michael and Stuart. But I was never really in the fight. He dominated me.

The fight in the gym started after I'd whacked Darren in the back of the head with the plastic shaft of my stick. I'd spent much of the year in the weight room, and I was four or five inches taller than Darren. But he attacked me ferociously, smothering me with a barrage of punches. He landed on top of me when we went to the ground and continued to pummel me. He felt like a mattress on top of me. I was blinded, arms and legs immobilized, while his fists kept raining down on my face, no matter where I turned.

I didn't think I'd landed one punch or even threw that many. My only response, while we were on the floor, was to claw at his face and pull on his hair. In those endless seconds when he had me mounted, defenseless, I thought about the repercussions of my crushing defeat, which rippled through me for many years.

He broke my nose. It wasn't hanging off of my face, but it didn't feel or sound right. When I inspected my nose in front of the upstairs bathroom mirror later that night, I could see that the cartilage in the tip of my nose had been dislodged. The septum was sloppy and uneven, and it clicked in and out of alignment when I touched it.

I removed a binder and the Math textbook from my locker, and then I closed the door and glared at him, forcing a smile, holding out my right hand then quickly withdrawing it. "Darren Clayton," I said, as if we were long-lost friends.

"Hey, egg," he said.

Egg was short for egghead, his nickname for me.

I had a large head. I was reminded of that when I looked into my locker mirror. It was long and wide. I couldn't put on a hat or wear headphones. Nothing fit. Darren was staring at my head. "You think I have a large head?" I asked him. "Just say it."

"Does your neck hurt having to carry that large cranium?" he asked me, with as much seriousness as he could muster.

I looked up and down the hallway. Although it was a relief to not see any teachers, they wouldn't have stopped me anyway. I threw a punch with my right hand that grazed Darren's chin. Then I lunged forward. I locked my hands around the back of his neck and landed a series of elbow and knee strikes. When I released him, he crumpled to the floor. Then I picked him up and tossed him toward his open locker. When I looked around, I saw several students holding yearbooks.

I walked down the hall and saw more students with yearbooks. When I moved into the side hallway, where the television was, I saw a stack of yearbooks on a table. I dropped a twenty-dollar note into the open cashbox and took a brand new copy of the 1991 yearbook off the top of the pile. I opened it right there and found Tracey's headshot.

As I turned the page, I looked down through the glass that extended around the upstairs floor. I saw Tracey. She was standing on a square, halfway between the smoke pit and the walkway, joined by Robin Daly and Shannon McKenzie.

I turned to the color picture of the three of them sitting in front of a row of lockers downstairs. When I looked down again, I saw Tracey leave Robin and Shannon and enter the school. I knew that she was headed in the direction of her locker.

When I entered Math class, I reclaimed my seat and then turned and looked into the back right corner of the classroom at Tracey's empty seat. She was always among the last to arrive.

I kept track of the rest of the students, one by one, as they arrived, based on everything I knew about the adults they'd become. There was an airline executive, a child care counselor, dance instructor, English professor, forklift operator, labor negotiator, a modeling agent, a snowboard-course designer, even a sommelier.

I could've laid out the future for all of them, which

would've been cruel and pointless. Was I going to tell Alicia Forrester that she'd die from a rare blood disease at the age of thirty-seven? No, but I knew that, and knowing so much about almost everyone around me made my heart leap into my throat every time I tried to respond to a simple hello or a nod.

When Tracey arrived, I watched her take her seat, and then I turned away and stared down at the yearbook on my desk.

The seat in front of Tracey was empty. It'd been formerly occupied by Morgan Bradbury, who'd left the class a few weeks earlier. They were a potent combination: Morgan's chestnut hair cascading down around her milky white shoulders, her emerald green eyes locked onto me, the two of them laughing at my shyness, whispering behind my back.

Chad Fletcher, Tracey's prom date, was three seats ahead of Tracey. In his future, his bangs had been eaten away by male pattern baldness, and he'd gotten very fat. I pictured his beefy fingers clasping a Red Bull, his lard ass squirming on a bar stool, sitting sideways, as he did in class, stretching his stubby legs to relieve some of the arthritis pain.

I first learned that Tracey was going to the prom with Chad when she approached Sandra Yang's desk one morning before class and gave Sandra, the grad cruise organizer, a check.

"Who are you going with?" she asked Tracey.

Tracey sighed. "Chad."

I stole a glance at Tracey before the class started.

I didn't know anything about her life.

After Mr. Phillips diagnosed several geometry problems on the chalkboard, he took his argyle shirt and turquoise pants back to his desk and opened his mark book. "Who still has to do their presentation?" he asked, looking around the class.

Tracey raised her hand. It was Friday, and the following week was the last week of classes, followed by the week of final exams.

"Who are you doing yours on, Tracey?" Phillips asked her from his chair.

I scribbled *Lewis Carroll* into the webbing of my binder. "Lewis Carroll," I whispered, a second before Tracey answered.

I watched her rise and walk to the front of the class. She laid her notes on the makeshift podium and then looked across the room. "Most of you probably know Lewis Carroll as the author of *Alice's Adventures in Wonderland*," she began, repeating the words I'd dwelled on and scrutinized since June 1991, "but Lewis Carroll also made several notable contributions to mathematics." I looked right at her. "As a mathematician," she continued, "Carroll worked in the areas of geometry, matrix algebra, mathematical logic, and recreational mathematics."

When she finished her presentation and left the podium, I thought I saw Chad leave his seat and meet her in the aisle.

I saw them kiss each other for a long time.

Chapter 6

Journalism, my second block class, was in the cafeteria, whose large window looked out onto the grassy slope we all stood on for the class picture.

I removed a copy of my last issue of the school newspaper, *The Phoenix*, from a holder and then made a beeline for the inconspicuous door in the corner of the room. The door, which faced the tables, stood between the cafeteria line and the window.

The shoebox-sized room behind that door was like an afterthought. It'd been grafted onto the cafeteria and had more in common with the forest and the trees than the rest of the school. There was only enough space in there for Ms. Novacek's desk, two rows of three tables, and a 1970s filling cabinet, where the back issues were buried.

Ms. Novacek, who I thought looked a little like a young Bo Derek, had a perpetual smile and a stripper's body. She told us that she'd been a Canadian Football League cheerleader in her early twenties, which didn't surprise me, and that she arrived at teaching after making a frank assessment of her appearance, her body, and her prospects.

In the first few days of the last semester, before Ms. Novacek handed out assignments for the first issue, she appeared as an enigma in front of me—a seemingly dumb blonde who talked about journalistic ethics, news gathering techniques, and the all-important square inches. She did this eloquently, and I found her to be much more credible than most of the other teachers at Moody.

With the last issue of *The Phoenix* completed, I couldn't think of a reason to stay until Helga Makkela sat down in front of me. She turned and smiled at me.

I graduated from Seaview with Helga. But she went to Moody Junior instead of Banting, after Helga, her mother, and Helga's younger sister moved away from the Woodlands. The next time I saw her was on the opening day of grade eleven, which was very awkward.

It was great to see her in front of me again, but I was in awe of her. I felt inadequate in her presence, embarrassed by how boring and incomplete my story had turned out compared to hers.

Helga's lengthy academic and professional career was fully documented on her LinkedIn page, which I checked periodically, though nothing in her career had really changed since October 2013, when Helga was made a partner at her Toronto law firm.

It was a corporate law firm, one of the most powerful in North America, and Helga handled acquisitions, loans, and mergers. She posted her thoughts online, mostly about legal issues, but also concerning grief. She lost her mother in 2010.

I found a 2012 picture of Helga attending a fashion gala in Toronto. She was wearing a low-cut dress in the picture, and she had a naughty expression on her face. The yellow hair I fondly remembered had turned platinum blonde.

The partnership announcement on the firm's website included a picture of Helga wearing a black robe and a white neck tab, standing with the rest of the associates who'd also been made partners, all men. She looked very formidable. She looked like a woman no one could mess with.

"Helga!" I said.

"I loved your article in the paper," she said, opening the last issue and pointing at my byline.

For the last issue, I'd written an article examining the films that had been released during our time at Moody Senior, between the fall of 1989 and the spring of 1991. I closed the article by stating that *The Silence of the Lambs,* which was released in February 1991, was the most overrated film of the period. I wrote that it was much inferior to the film *Manhunter*, which was released in 1986 and was the first film in which the Hannibal Lecter character appeared.

"I was an idiot," I said, cringing at my words. "What was I thinking?"

"No, you were right on," Helga insisted. "If *Silence of the Lambs* wins any Oscars, I'll puke."

"I think *Manhunter* is a better film," I said, "but I like *Silence of the Lambs*. The most overrated film of this era? That's silly. What about *Home Alone*?"

That statement clearly irked Rachel Beckett, who sat in the opposite row, against the wall. "*Home Alone* is my favorite movie," she chirped.

"You're a moron," I said to her.

Rachel Beckett would later run the student services department at Simon Fraser University.

"It's great to see you," I said to Helga. "I'm so proud of you."

She leaned over the divide, face brightening, jubilant. "I like you," she said, voice trembling. "God, I said it. I like you. I've had a crush on you forever."

"It would've been nice to have had that information back in, say, grade six," I said.

"Do you want to go to the prom?" she asked me, spitting out the words, needing to catch her breath before she could finish the thought. "Together."

On prom night, toward the end of the night, I'd looked around the Plaza of Nations, the site of the prom, for Helga, determined to dance with someone. But I couldn't find her anywhere, and I didn't remember her being there in the evening. I never saw her again.

"You didn't go to the prom, did you?" I asked her, struggling to maintain any semblance of context, losing track of time. "You're not going to the prom, are you?" I hastily corrected.

"Do you want to go with me?" she said, nearly begging.

"Oh, Helga," I said, voice cracking. "I'd love to, and I'd be so lucky to have you with me, but there's someone else I've been waiting for, all of my life, and I need to ask her."

She flashed me an understanding smile, and then she nodded and turned away from me.

୧ჟ୧ჟ

After I left the cafeteria, with more than thirty minutes left in second block, I went upstairs and found Michael and Stuart in the gym, shooting hoops.

I caught them by surprise when I ran into the gym. After I intercepted the ball from them, I dribbled around the perimeter and then through the paint. I stopped just inside the free throw line then let go a teardrop that almost fell straight down through the hole.

I thought playing basketball in grade twelve would transform me, in and out of school. But it was a disappointment. Because I hadn't played in grade eleven, I wasn't viewed as a true senior by the other players, and I spent far too much time on the bench for me to feel part of a team. I was a glorified water boy, and just as Michael and Stuart transferred the confidence they displayed on the court to the rest of their lives, I remained trapped at the end of the bench.

"I'd give anything to play another year," I said, tossing the ball to Michael.

"What do you want to do tonight?" Michael asked me and Stuart.

"Is there a party?" Stuart asked Michael, not me.

"Probably at Rex's," Michael said.

Rex Heglund was the most popular guy at school. His appeal crossed all boundaries. He charmed the teachers, and he always made time for the bottom dwellers, a group I wasn't many steps removed from.

On the evening of Boxing Day 1991, Rex would be belted to the backseat of a car that struck a power pole in Coquitlam. Asleep, he would be killed instantly. A memorial bursary would be established in his name.

I took the ball and dribbled beyond the three-point line. The door I'd entered through opened behind me just as the ball left my fingers.

I watched the ball swoosh through the hoop, and then I turned and saw Coach, Mr. Rockwell, standing in the doorway, clutching his precious stack of keys.

"Where was that this season?" he asked me, looking impressed.

"It was on the bench," I said.

♋♋

When I left the gym, through the other door, I saw Morgan Bradbury in front of me. She was roving the long hallway where my locker was, enjoying her second free block in a row after ditching Math. She was wearing the black-and-white polka dot blouse and light blue skinny jeans I saw whenever she haunted my dreams. Her white skin turned pink when she saw me. Then she flashed that mischievous smile.

No girl had expressed interest in me as openly as Morgan had since Lisa Dionne told me she loved me at Seaview, back in the second grade. Lisa moved away the following year, before we even kissed. When she reappeared at Moody, she had a boyfriend, which told me that the pledge she'd made to me in the Seaview cloakroom had either been forgotten or retracted.

I met Morgan for the first time in the last semester of grade eleven, in the back of the school office one morning before the start of classes, during a career counseling session that was presided over by Mrs. Whitlow, my designated counselor.

Morgan sat across from me at the narrow table, and I

felt her presence immediately, while I pretended to listen to Mrs. Whitlow explain our various career options, which included the funeral services industry.

Morgan and I were joined at the table by five or six other purposeless souls. As we all, one by one, tried to articulate our confusion to Mrs. Whitlow, I saw in Morgan's expression—and heard in her frightened voice—that she was genuinely lost. Her face became as malleable as putty as she tried to explain why she did not have the faintest idea of what she wanted to do with the rest of her life.

I felt Morgan's stare for the first time when it was my turn to speak, and I could see that she was clearly attracted to me. The attraction, which was mutual, turned out to be purely physical. We never exchanged a single word.

Besides the one counseling session I attended, and Math, Morgan and I were in the same History class in the first semester of grade twelve. She sat directly in front of me on the first day, which was my last day in the class. She glanced back at me repeatedly then whispered to the girl beside her, who turned to me and said, "She likes you."

One day in 2004, inspired by a mixture of boredom and curiosity, I did an online search for Morgan, which revealed that she was living in New York. She worked at the United Nations, where Morgan—who completed a master's degree in Political Science in Toronto, specializing in Gender and International Relations—developed and spearheaded global initiatives to end violence against girls and women.

Morgan Bradbury at the United Nations! I couldn't believe it. When I saw that, I tried to replace the old Morgan with the new one: I had her walking around in ballet flats, wearing a black pin-striped two-button blazer with solid gray pants. Then I put organic makeup on her face and pulled a lightweight cashmere V-neck sweater around her slim body. But I couldn't see any of it.

❧❦❧

I had an open block after Journalism, followed by Creative Writing with Mr. Elson, which was easily my favorite of all of my classes at Moody. I had Social Studies with Mr. Rockwell in fifth block, which was an open block for Tracey.

I visited Creative Writing in block four, just to see the late Mr. Elson, who'd given me an A in his class, the only A I received at Moody, and told me I had a fertile imagination. I stayed with him for fifteen minutes, and then I went downstairs and staked out Tracey's locker from the end of the hall.

She arrived at her locker a few minutes before the end of fourth block. She removed a bag from the locker, and then she closed the door and walked through the nearest hallway exit, headed toward the smoke pit and the walkway.

I stopped in front of the door and looked out at her. Then I turned to my left and stared at the top of the hill, at the upper parking lot, where I knew she was ultimately headed. I'd done this before.

After exchanging a few words with the smoke pit crowd, she reentered the school through the door on the opposite side of the walkway, headed in the direction of the cafeteria and the school office. She made a brief stop in the cafeteria, where she found Robin and Shannon, and then she left the cafeteria and walked down the adjoining hallway, past the teachers' lounge, into the back of the school office, where she met with her counselor for ten minutes.

When she left the office, I thought she might simply walk out the door to the front of the school and go directly to the parking lot. But she instead entered the stairwell and walked upstairs. She went in and out of the library, and then she turned the corner and walked down the side hallway that ended at the English Lit classroom, where I'd first laid eyes on her.

She turned right at the intersection in front of the English Lit door and walked past my locker, down the long hallway.

I ran to the end of the hall, facing the gym, and turned left. When I looked into the side hallway, she was gone.

I ran around the corner. When I reached the door and looked out, I saw her back entering the lot, just before she disappeared behind the cars.

I pushed the door open and ran after her. When I reached the edge of the parking lot, I couldn't see her at first. The neighboring forest was bearing down on me, and the overhanging branches shaded most of the cars.

Then I heard her crisp, rapid-fire steps, too many to count. I moved past a long truck and found her behind it. She was standing next to a gray sedan. I took long steps toward her and stopped five feet away, to the left of her.

"Tracey," I said.

She slowly turned around. Her face was completely expressionless, eyes betraying nothing, neither encouraging me nor pushing me away. I stepped forward.

"Hi," she said, smiling.

Whenever she smiled, her abdomen and chest contracted as the electrical current ran through her. The light escaped through her eyes and mouth.

"We were in English Lit last semester," I said. "Do you remember?"

She nodded. "We sat next to each other."

"We sure did," I said. "I really liked your presentation on Lewis Carroll."

"Thank you," she said, starting to blush.

"Why did you pick Lewis Carroll?" I asked, really wanting to know.

"I loved his books as a kid," she said.

"Did you know he was a photographer?" I asked her.

"I read that somewhere."

"He took pictures for over twenty years," I said. "He was a gentleman photographer. He created over 3,000 images. He liked to photograph young girls."

"Wow," she said. "You seem to know a lot about him."

"I'm a photographer," I said.

She opened the driver's side door and dropped her bag inside. I only had the yearbook with me.

"Did you want to talk to me about Lewis Carroll?" she asked.

I leaned in closer to her. Any closer and we would've had to either dance or kiss. "I want your phone number," I said.

I opened the yearbook and turned to Tracey's headshot. I couldn't find a pen. She had one. She laid the yearbook down on the hood and wrote her phone number along the margin, beside her face.

She handed the yearbook back to me. I held the door open and watched her slide into the driver's seat. Before I closed the door, I looked around the interior and inhaled. I caught a whiff of Chanel No. 5.

She lowered the window and looked at me.

Chapter 7

I stared at Tracey's phone number in my yearbook all the way home in Michael's car. My fingers traced over the neat, upward slants and strokes, while I gazed lovingly at the pressure she'd applied to the page.

I knew there was a very good chance that Dad would be waiting for me when I arrived home. He routinely left his office early on Fridays, and he usually stopped off at one of the video stores on the way home, either Crazy Mike's Video or Rogers Video.

He always seemed to pick the worst movies that were available in the New Releases section.

When Michael and Stuart dropped me off in front of the house, I avoided looking at the driveway. I looked at Michael and Stuart as if I was never going to see them again, and I tried to extend our conversation as long as possible before I had to let them go.

"You think your Dad might let you take the Bimmer out?" Michael asked me, pointing at the driveway. "It's a special occasion."

"Speaking of which," Stuart said, "we have to pay for the limo next week."

"Limo, prom, cruise, party," Michael said, rattling off our planned itinerary for prom night on his fingers. "We're never going home."

When there was nothing more left to be said, I waved goodbye to them and watched the Mustang drive away. I stared up the hill until it was out of sight and I could no longer hear the flutter of the chrome rims, the grating of the turbine wheels.

Then I turned and saw Dad's BMW. Brad's Jeep Wrangler was parked in the corner of the large driveway, near Mom's prizzed flower garden.

I circled the BMW, sliding my left hand along the driver's side door and then over the warm hood.

I never drove the BMW unless Dad was with me. Whenever I inquired about the possibility of taking the BMW out by myself, Dad gently refused. The main reason he gave me was that I wasn't insured to drive it, although he never lifted a finger toward adding me to his insurance.

When I reached the front door, I pulled out my house key and dangled it in front of the lock. I slammed the door shut when I walked inside, and then my feet trampled the hallway rug. I stood on the rug and waited until I heard Dad's footsteps from the living room.

I closed my eyes at first, listening to his footsteps. Then I stared down at the rug, waiting until his feet stopped just short of me, behind the cinnamon cologne I could smell a mile away.

I hadn't seen him so happy since the night of my high school graduation. He was, again, hopeful for the future and proud of me, though my most impressive achievement, up until that point, was being spelling bee champion at Seaview.

Dad's belief in me and my potential didn't die easily. By the end of 1995, when it was clear that I was no longer attending classes at Simon Fraser University, SFU, and was about to leave the school altogether, Dad rationalized that the business administration track I'd been on simply wasn't a good fit for me. He convinced himself, Mom, and me that it was just a matter of time before I found something I was passionate about.

But I disconnected myself from the outside world instead. As my withdrawal became more and more disturbing and pronounced, Dad slowly began to adjust and lower his expectations and goals for me. It got to the point where he wanted nothing more than for me to find a job and get out of the house.

One Friday night in 1996, I came home after midnight

and heard Dad crying upstairs. We didn't, as far as I knew, have any living relatives outside of College Park, so my first thought was that Brad, who'd moved out in 1993, had been killed. But when I listened at the bottom of the stairs, I heard Dad and Mom commiserating over their failure with me. "What did we do wrong?" I heard Dad ask Mom, sobbing. "What's going to happen to him?"

I tried to kill myself three times in 1996, in the aftermath of leaving university and losing touch with my friends. These halfhearted attempts involved my bedroom radio, sleeping pills from the Shoppers Drug Mart at Burquitlam Plaza, and a brown belt from my closet.

I dumped the radio into the upstairs bathroom sink one day, while my right hand was underwater. Nothing happened, not even to the radio, which was only temporarily disabled. I swallowed an entire bottle of sleeping pills, twice, up in my bedroom, downing them with milk. I fell into bed afterward, expecting to slip into a coma. But the pills didn't even knock me out, after taking so many in such a short period of time.

The pills left me blind and numb. I was fully conscious of my other senses, which became wildly amplified. When I gently tapped my teeth together, the sound echoed through my ears.

I thought about my parents, one or both, discovering my corpse in bed, and then I wondered what everyone else would say and think about me, then and years later. I was still in denial about how alone and forgotten I truly was.

I tried to hang myself with the belt in the backyard, outside the sliding glass door, but when I slipped my head through the opening, and kicked the chair I was standing on away, the belt snapped immediately. My back hit the cement hard, which was the only physical pain I felt from all of this.

"Hey, pal," Dad said, holding a copy of the *Tri-City News*. "I'm going to call Pizza Hut."

I heard Brad's movement upstairs and music from his bedroom. When Dad pointed into the living room, I couldn't see the stack of video rentals, but I knew exactly what I'd find. "I stopped off at the video store on the way home and got some movies," he said. "Good ones."

Before Dad retired, I'd established a routine around looking after Mom that gave me a fragile sense of structure, even as I transitioned from my late-twenties to my early-thirties, beaten and tired, old beyond my years.

When Dad retired, he assumed most of my responsibilities with Mom, which left me reeling. With Dad home, my job was to put Mom on the commode when he wasn't present, empty her bedpan at night, and give her the nightly pills, which Dad meticulously cut up into halves and quarters and then placed on a glass tray for me.

But by that time, I couldn't seem to do anything right in his eyes. As careful as I was with giving Mom her eight o'clock pills with water, Dad sometimes found coughed up pills on the bed, or on the carpet. "These pills are for her blood pressure," he would say to me, holding an undigested orange or yellow pill in front of me. "If she doesn't take her pills, she could have another stroke. Do you want to kill your mother?"

I couldn't remember whether I'd even spoken to Dad the last time I'd returned home from school on June 7, 1991. This time, in the hallway, I wrapped my arms around him, which was the first time I'd touched him since I'd stood over him in the funeral home. I gave him a big, crushing hug. I held onto him far longer than was normal, which was by design. I wanted to force him to pry me off of him, which was what happened. "Are you feeling okay?" he asked me.

"I love you, Dad," I said. "I've missed you so much."

"Well, that's nice to hear," he said, "but it hasn't been that long, has it?"

I examined him closely. Until I'd seen Mom again in my bedroom, I'd forgotten what she looked like in her past life. The last years of her life left such an indelible impression on me that it made me feel as if I'd had two mothers—which was very strange.

It was the same with Dad, mostly because of how estranged we'd been before he died. I couldn't find a trace of gray or silver on his head in the hallway, although my fingers didn't dig very deep below the surface. He was forty-eight in June 1991.

"I forgot what you looked like, Dad," I said.

Dad saw the yearbook in my right hand and pulled it away from me before I could react. He flipped through it. He stopped at my yearbook picture and looked at my black-and-white face. Then his eyes moved down to my brief inscription.

They didn't give us much time to compose our ending thoughts, just a few minutes with a piece of paper, which I guessed was supposed to induce spontaneity, but often resulted in stupidity, as I'd proved with my inscription. I'd written *The Evil is Gone*, inspired by a line of dialogue from the film *Halloween*.

Mom, who was born in Australia and went to Canada when she was sixteen, left behind no evidence of her young life, except for Aloysius Hunchback Witt. That was the name she'd given me when I'd inquired about her first boyfriends, not including Albert Finney and William Holden.

When I combed through the basement bookshelf in 2015, I found Dad's school dance booklet from 1961, the year he graduated from Burnaby North High, which no longer existed. When I opened the thin booklet, the most telling aspect, besides the sight of my father's teenage handwriting, was the name Pat Downey, which Dad had recorded over and over again.

I saw her in Dad's 1961 senior yearbook, which I found in the kitchen, in the underneath cabinet between the fridge and the sink, under the maps and phone books. She had an open face with a prominent forehead and wore her short light brown hair in a pixie cut. She was wearing a simple pearl necklace and pearl earrings. The pearls matched her upper teeth, which were barely visible in her impish, unrepentant smile.

There was a shallow layer of fog over her face, as if she had faded a bit every time Dad thought about her.

Dad turned to the basketball team picture. He smiled at the sight of me and the guys bunched together on the bottom row. Then he focused on me, in the middle, holding the basketball. I quickly slid my left hand across the picture and turned the page. "Dad, can you keep a secret?" I asked him. *Dad, you and Mom are on the mantel.*

"What is it?" he asked.

I took back the yearbook and flipped over to Tracey's headshot. I showed the picture to him, pointing at her face, waiting for his reaction.

He calmly scanned her face, and then he turned to me and nodded. "She's a pretty girl," he said, pointing at her phone number on the page. Then he tickled my ribs. "Are you taking her to the prom?"

"I'm going to spend the rest of my life with her," I said.

⌘

I walked upstairs and tapped on Brad's door, but the music inside was too loud for him to hear me, so I pushed the door open without permission.

When I walked into his room, I found him slouched over his bed, between the sheets, surrounded by some of the same *Dungeons & Dragons* paraphernalia I'd seen in the box he'd tried to remove from the house. He was reading an issue of *Dragon*, the magazine that was the bible of fantasy role-playing.

I stepped over an apron from a Chinese restaurant in downtown Port Moody, recalling the end of Brad's time at the University of British Columbia. "You dropped out," I said.

"The faculty told me to take a year off," he said, without a trace of optimism in his voice. "I can go back."

Brad had been enrolled in the engineering program at UBC, where the engineering students were notorious for executing outrageous pranks every year. In Brad's freshman year, they hung a Volkswagen Beetle atop the school's clock tower, which resulted in several students being expelled.

After the prank had been executed, Brad insisted that he'd been involved, but when I and some of Brad's friends pressed him for details, he was suspiciously vague. After we kept on him, he finally admitted that he'd played no role in it.

Early in his sophomore year at UBC, Brad, like many others, started to become overwhelmed by the intensifying demands of the coursework. Unfortunately, this led him to follow in our mother's footsteps and become a real estate agent. That career didn't require a brain, just a stack of business cards and the phony smile he inherited from Mom.

"Maybe engineering's not for you," I said, trying to overlay a goatee and pot belly onto Brad's lithe figure, without much success.

"Don't tell Mom," he pleaded. "She'll be pissed."

Brad tossed a *D&D* module at me. When I opened it, I saw Brad's hand-drawn, intricate maps attached to the pages. "What's this one about?" I asked, pointing at the dungeon maps, standing between the front edge of his bed and the doorway.

"It takes place in the Forgotten Realms," he said. "You'll be running into liches, if you think you're ready for that."

When I stopped playing *D&D* in the early nineties, I was a third-level fighter, and I'd worked very hard to get that far. Brad could've turned me into Conan or Thor with a flick of his wrist, but he was the kind of Dungeon Master who loathed taking shortcuts. He insisted that his players earn every experience point they received, even if it meant killing a battalion of goblins in one sitting, which was time consuming but not terribly difficult. Goblins were the commonest and weakest race of monsters in the *D&D* universe, tailor-made for low-level players wanting to gain easy experience points and build their self-confidence.

The one break Brad gave me was with my character's weakest attribute, his intelligence, which had a rating of four, out of a possible eighteen. Fighters, who were aspiring barbarians, weren't the sharpest steak knives in the drawer to begin with, and a four meant that my character was, essentially, a vegetable.

This became an endless source of laughter for the rest of the players who sat at the table with us down in the basement. They wondered if my fighter might be susceptible to hypnosis and mind control through simple eye contact. I endured the joking, stoically, not wanting to weaken my other attributes—constitution, dexterity, strength—to bolster my intelligence. But when the joking continued, with no end in sight, Brad finally relented and, with the toss of a die, raised my intelligence to a six. Suddenly, I was a high-functioning basket case.

I closed the module and tossed it onto the bed. "Somebody has to teach those fuckers a lesson," I said, and then I walked out.

When I entered my room, I flopped down on the bed with the hard, sturdy copy of the 1991 yearbook I'd bought earlier that day at school. The revitalized edges of the yearbook dug into my ribs and left red marks on my stomach.

I turned on the radio and listened to Zed. Every song I heard was connected to grade twelve. The Divinyls' "I Touch Myself" transported me down to the basement on June 28, 1991, in the early evening.

I was watching the raunchy video for the song on MuchMusic in my prom tuxedo, waiting for Michael and

Stuart, who arrived with the limousine just after the video ended.

On the night I was battered by Darren Clayton in the school gym, Pet Shop Boys' "West End Girls" was the first song I heard when I returned home and entered my room.

I opened the yearbook and turned to Tracey's headshot. I was relieved when I saw that her phone number was still there on the page. I once again admired her handwriting, which was so noble and upright compared to my horrid penmanship.

Then I sat up and looked at the phone on the dresser directly in front of me. I picked up the phone, pausing for several beats before I dialed Tracey's number, which I'd already memorized. I had to wait eight rings before Tracey answered, in a somewhat breathless state. She sounded as if she'd just gotten out of the shower.

"Hello," she said, not in the form of a question, which I took as a good sign.

"It's Ryan," I said. "I don't think I told you my name in the parking lot, did I?"

"I know who you are," she said. "Ryan Tremblay. Is your family French?"

I recalled Dad mentioning that our family name had originally been Chittle and that my great-grandfather changed it to Tremblay after he fled England, for reasons unknown to me. He migrated to the Canadian Prairies in the late-nineteenth century.

"I don't think so," I said. "I never heard my father speak a word of French in his life. He's about as French as Saskatchewan sealskin."

"So we're going to the prom," she said.

"You'd better believe it," I said. "Hey, there's a question I forgot to ask you."

"What?"

"Do you know how beautiful you are?"

"Why do you think I'm beautiful?"

I could have spent the rest of my life trying to describe what happened to me on that first day in English Lit, the first day of classes in grade twelve, when I looked to my right and saw Tracey for the first time.

I was in the back left corner of the classroom, in front of the door. Tracey was on the other side of the class, against the wall, sitting diagonally opposite me. I could only see the back of her head and the left side of her face from where I was sitting, but I was immediately drawn to her.

She was wearing a sleeveless white tank top with a bra, and tight jeans hugged her curves. The sway of her hips was hypnotic. The summer had coated her porcelain skin with warm caramel and yellowed her silky blonde hair.

After my first sighting of her, excitement buzzed inside me, which I was sure had nothing to do with the start of senior year. When I returned home from school that day, I went straight upstairs to my bedroom, to the yearbook drawer, to find her—her face, and her name, which was unknown to me, until I looked down, into the 1990 yearbook, and saw her grade eleven picture.

"Tracey," I said to her picture, first wondering what the reason was for the unconventional spelling of her name. Then I hugged myself on the edge of the bed, realizing that Tracey had become a holy name, the most wonderful name in the world.

A couple of days later, she took the seat beside me on my left.

"Do you want to go out tonight?" I asked her, the phone cord twisting around my right index finger, turning it purple.

Chapter 8

For my date with Tracey, my first date and hers, I wore a white cotton and polyester shirt and gray Dockers pants. The buttoned shirt sagged over my shoulders, so I tucked it in deep and inserted a black belt through the loops. I tightened the belt until it felt like there was a tourniquet around my gut.

Mom, who bought all of my clothes throughout high school, bought the pants and shirt for me in grade ten, for the band concerts. But she always had girls in mind when she picked out my clothes. "Do you like girls?" she'd once asked me.

Before I went downstairs, I brushed my teeth and combed my hair in front of the bathroom mirror. Then I confronted my nose hairs.

As bothersome and disgusting as my nose hairs were, they were canny and resourceful, and I gave them grudging admiration for evading my most determined efforts to end them.

My lopsided nose gave the hairs maximum exposure, regardless of whether they were inside my nose or dangling out. They were thick buggers, which made removing them with tweezers a bloody painful option, so I turned to the scissors.

Of all of the cosmetic and physical changes I felt and witnessed on my return to 1991, I was most unprepared for the restoration of lightness throughout my body. At first, I thought this was simply a result of being a teenager again. But when I opened my mouth in front of the mirror, I realized that it was mostly because of my teeth.

My teeth weren't pearly white in 1991. They were crooked and rickety, but I didn't have to continually manage the cavities, faded enamel, and loose fillings that plagued me well into my forties.

There was no need, when I was eighteen, for Advil or Oral B rinses, and the headaches were gone. I didn't wince at all as the Listerine swam through my mouth and coated my gums, and the floss didn't get entangled in plaque when I slid it back and forth.

I stopped going to the dentist when I fell off Dad's coverage in 1996, and I made no attempt to go back. Although basic medical coverage was a birthright in Canada, dental care was a definite luxury. But it was embarrassment that prevented me from seeing a dentist again for nearly twenty years.

No woman would've enjoyed kissing me.

I'd never kissed a girl.

✁✁

Whenever I entered the living room, after Dad died, I invariably gravitated toward the mantel. When I arrived downstairs and stared at the mantel, before I left the house and went to Tracey's house, my eyes were dry and still. Then my heart started racing, scorching my chest, forcing me to loosen the buttons on my shirt until the top of my ribcage was exposed.

I turned and saw Mom in the hallway. I walked out of the living room to meet her, buttoning up my shirt and brushing my hair with my hands. She almost burst out laughing when she saw the pants and shirt I was wearing. Then she eyed me top to bottom.

"You look nice," she said, leaning in to sniff my armpits. "You combed your hair."

Dad walked out of the kitchen and kissed Mom on both cheeks. "Going out with the boys?" he asked me, winking, holding the case for *Spaced Invaders*, the first movie he planned to watch that night, after I was gone.

"Yeah, the usual," I said, looking for an exit point, prepared to run out the door without explanation if necessary. "See you later."

"Is Brad upstairs?" Mom asked both of us, just as I reached for the door.

"Yes," I said, pointing upstairs, "and he told me he's doing great at UBC."

"That's great news," Mom said. "Listen, honey, I know I keep on you, but I was just wondering if you have any idea about what you want to do after high school?"

I knew the career I should've chosen after high school, which was a bitter pill to swallow, because the choices I made when I was eighteen set the course for the rest of my life. By the time I realized what I'd done to myself, I thought it was too late to do anything about it. But it wasn't. I could've made the correction when I was twenty-five, even later than that. I simply dropped out of the world.

I should've become a sportscaster. I was a walking sports almanac, and when I talked about sports, which I could do forever, my comments were clear and incisive. This was my calling.

I should've enrolled in the broadcast communications program at the British Columbia Institute of Technology, BCIT, after graduating from Moody Senior. BCIT produced many radio and television personalities over the years, including Gloria Lim, who graduated from Moody in 1992. She co-anchored the evening news on BCTV. I watched her almost every evening.

"I want to be a doctor," I said, looking at Mom with a deadpan expression.

She rocked back on her heels, taking sluggish breaths. After digesting the unexpected announcement, she broke into a smile and wrapped her arms around me. "That's wonderful," she said. "Dad and I will support you all the way through university and medical school. We'll even buy you a new car. I'm so happy."

"Goodbye," I said, turning away from them and opening the door.

ᏇᎧᏇᎧ

I stopped in front of my car and looked around the neighborhood. Babysitters were arriving at houses, and couples were leaving College Park for the night. Two teenagers I didn't recognize were standing in front of the bus stop just down the street from my house. They were scrambling for change and straddling the curb. I heard playful echoes from Westhlll Park.

The sky was lemony white and showed no signs of yielding to darkness. I couldn't recall the last Friday that had seemed so obedient and receptive to my wishes. My last positive experience with a Friday happened in 2013, when I discovered, by accident, that several pictures of mine had been included in an issue of *Real Weddings*.

I stared at the chrome bat out of hell, trying to make

amends after our long separation. I began by apologizing for the abhorrent treatment she'd received from me during our final years together.

My Honda Civic finally bit the dust in 2002, and I had neither the ability nor the desire to replace her. I became a recluse. Without a car, I felt the presence of an invisible barrier that dropped out of the sky. I only left College Park, and rode the buses that ran constantly in both directions outside the house, to cash the quarterly low income tax credit checks, which was my only source of income after Dad retired.

The driver's side door creaked like a dormant treasure chest when I opened it. "We went through a lot together, old girl, didn't we?" I whispered as I held the door open and looked inside, waiting for a reply.

Just then a red Chevette pulled into the driveway. I knew the teenager who got out of the car, holding a pizza bag. It was Jason Rinaldo, one of my favorite people at school, outside of Michael, Stuart, and Tracey. I considered Jason a school friend.

Desperate to expand my social reach at Moody beyond Michael and Stuart, I'd bonded with Jason through our mutual love of boxing, a sport that attracted only a miniscule following at Moody. On October 25, 1990, Jason and I went out to watch the heavyweight title fight between James "Buster" Douglas and Evander Holyfield. It was the only time in high school I went out with anyone but Michael and

Stuart, whose friendship, from Seaview to Moody, was the only thing that kept me from being an outcast.

That evening, Jason picked me up outside our school in his small commuter car, and then we headed west, to the city of New Westminster, home to Douglas College, where I spent two unproductive years. We drove past the college, up the steepest hill in British Columbia, on our way to a restaurant, where the pay-per-view event was shown on a big screen.

We watched the main event, and the undercard fights, inside the restaurant's lounge area, where it was standing room only. Although Jason was beside me, on my right, throughout, the lounge was so loud and packed that we could only hear each other by screaming. He nudged my right shoulder as Douglas, who was grossly overweight, and Holyfield finally entered the ring. We exchanged a high-five after Holyfield, who was my favorite boxer, knocked Douglas out in the third round.

My strategy with Jason didn't work. Although we remained on cordial terms at school, the only time I saw him again outside of school hours—other than graduation and the prom, and the night he arrived at my house with the pizza—was at the ill-fated Friday night ball hockey game in the gym. He saw everything.

After Darren and I were separated, I walked over to Jason and asked him how he thought I'd fared. "I think you lost," he told me, and then he joined Darren, which was when I realized that he belonged to my worst enemy.

"Hey," he said to me on his way to the front door. He stopped and set the bag down on the hood of my car.

"Jason!" I said, a bit breathless. "How's it going, man?"

After Moody, Jason, who would marry a doctor, would go to medical school at UBC and become a reproductive endocrinologist, a fertility specialist. He'd run a successful clinic in Vancouver and make frequent television appearances, where I'd see him with thick glasses and a goatee similar to Brad's.

I heard, on June 7, 1991, in my driveway, the reassuring voice that everyone wanted to hear in a doctor, especially the anxious, childless women Jason would eventually encounter daily. "Just working," Jason said. "Hey, do you still work up at the Petro-Can?"

I'd completely forgotten that I was supposed to be working at the Petro-Can on Saturday and Sunday. The thought filled me with joy.

"Yes," I said. "I work tomorrow, with the guys."

"Going somewhere special?" Jason asked me, seeing me without a jacket. It was perfect out, not too cold or warm, but with my propensity to sweat, I knew I had to pace myself, especially around Tracey. "You look smooth," he added.

"I've got a date," I proclaimed, looking at Jason, adding the glasses and goatee.

His eyes widened. "Great," he said, sounding amazed.

The front door opened, and Jason and I both looked at Dad, who opened his wallet, beckoning Jason, who nodded at me and then carried the bag, which contained four medium triple crowns, over to Dad. "Give him a big tip," I said to Dad, and then I fell into the driver's seat and closed the door.

I stopped in front of the College Park border and looked around before I made the left turn and drove to Tracey's house.

Over at Westhill Park, a family was playing touch football around the middle of the field, surrounded by kids throwing a Frisbee. The swimming pool was set to open at the end of June.

The lot on my right was still vacant but had been paved and zoned for the construction of the shiny new houses, the first of which appeared in 1992.

In the early-to-mid-1980s, the lot was occupied by a strip plaza whose chief tenant—after the other businesses, which had included a Royal Bank branch, fled the location—was a Mac's convenience store. The store's arcade games—my favorites were *Elevator Action, Frogger*, and *Karate Champ*—were a magnet for my friends and me. They also attracted regenerating, zombie-like delinquents, who buzzed around the store and the unpatrolled lot day and night.

They would melt into the patch of yellow grass and

weeds behind the store whenever they saw too many adults around.

Opposite the lot, and the park and the swimming pool, was an affordable housing square that was not quite a slum. There were several rapes and stabbings.

The future residents of College Park, those who weren't there in the eighties, wouldn't have believed me if I'd told them that their utopia was once a bloody, shadowy badlands where children weren't allowed to walk the night streets alone.

Chapter 9

After I reached the bottom of Snake Hill, I drove past Albert Street, the school, and then I moved into St. Johns Street, Port Moody's main artery. As I headed toward downtown Port Moody, I noticed a swirling orange hue in the sky watching over me, and I adopted it as a beacon. It approached from the north, where Tracey had told me her house was located during our phone conversation, which lasted just over three minutes.

Port Moody, which promoted itself as the City of the Arts in 2015, was a pass-through town in 1991. The first two blocks along St. Johns, which spanned five blocks in total, were lined with old houses that enjoyed landmark status by 2015. Downtown Port Moody in 1991 consisted only of three blocks of storefronts, small businesses. That was it.

The first place I stopped along St. Johns was the Shell station, which would still be there in 2015. As I was filling my car's small fuel tank, I looked to the right of the Shell station, toward the sloping site at the end of the block. The imposing one-and-one-half story building that towered over the site in 1991 was City Hall, which was built in 1914, the year after Port Moody was incorporated. The building was located squarely in the heart of Port Moody. It was the only spot in Port Moody where City Hall belonged.

After I filled the tank, I looked ahead to the following block, where I saw the Maple Florist storefront, which would also be still around in 2015.

Then I stood on the adjacent sidewalk and looked eastward toward the Port Moody Public Library, which was two blocks away. I couldn't quite see it.

A Royal Bank branch was located diagonally across the street from the Shell station. After I vacuumed my car's interior, I opened my wallet and found my bank card. I ran across the street and entered the bank, fully intending to empty my savings account before the end of June.

Then I bought a dozen roses.

❧❧❧

I believed that I could always sense exactly when and where Port Moody began and ended. This was sorely tested during my search for Tracey's house.

After leaving downtown Port Moody, I continued eastward until I reached Port Moody's eastern border, which was indicated by frail black letters on a plywood sheet.

I turned left and entered Ioco, an area of Port Moody named after the Imperial Oil Company, which built a refinery on the north shore of the Burrard Inlet in 1914. The refinery commenced operations in 1915, and by 1917, there were 200 people living in Ioco, which then consisted of some cabins, huts, and a grocery store that only accepted company currency.

As I followed Ioco Road, I glanced to my left toward the Ioco Recreation Center. I was overjoyed at the sight of the open space on its right, which became home to City Hall and the Port Moody Public Library. This was a crime.

Putting City Hall and the library there, which happened in 1995, made no geographic sense, since over ninety percent of Port Moody was located west of Ioco. It was only when Port Moody's boundaries were redrawn, which was accomplished through the creation of master-planned communities that the minority, vile carpetbaggers, were empowered to remake Port Moody in their image, which was most clearly represented in their gaping, glassy, overbuilt domicile.

When I last checked the Port Moody website, I saw that the majority of the city council members lived in outlying planned communities, boutique neighborhoods with deceptively unaffected-sounding names like Heritage Woods,

Klahanie, Newport Village, Noons Creek, and my personal favorite: Pleasantside.

I took a deep breath when I reached the first traffic light, facing the northern end of Port Moody, my car resting at the foot of Eagle Mountain, also known as Eagle Ridge, a mountainous ridge that brushed against Coquitlam. Anmore, the village municipality Tracey lived in, was nestled between the lower slopes of Eagle Mountain and the eastern shore of Indian Arm, a saltwater fjord that extended north from the Burrard Inlet.

Before Tracey told where she lived over the phone, I'd only ever heard of Anmore from Mom, who uttered the name with hallowed reverenced and coveted the rare listings.

I saw, in 1991, a semi-wilderness community that vigilantly guarded its independence and rural character by repelling the encroachment of urban development from its borders.

When my groaning car entered Anmore, which would have a population of less than 2,000 in 2015, I was greeted by a chorus of red-legged frogs and a huddle of roads and trails.

My imagination swelled with ideas about Tracey's parents. I decided that Tracey's parents—Tracey's father was a stockbroker in 1991, and her mother was a psychiatrist—chose to live in Anmore because they were self-sufficient people who were willing to assume absolute responsibility for their lives. I also speculated that they probably harbored some level of mistrust toward the federal government.

The trouble with making assumptions about people was that one guess always led to another, and the slightest mis-calculation was enough to cause the entire chain to shatter.

Projecting a teenage girl as a woman involved too many variables, and I was very wrong about Tracey, the woman, who'd long ceased to be the meek, unconfident girl I was with on the night of June 7, 1991.

I drove past a billboard with a detailed map of the small region pasted on it. When I saw that Tracey's street was nearby, the flesh between my Adam's apple turned flabby and moist. Sweat formed around my neck, and then it ran down my back.

Chapter 10

I found Tracey's house, which spanned more than 6,100 square feet, inside a seven-house cul-de-sac, which overlooked rolling hills that were peppered with fir trees.

Tracey's house, which was the biggest of the seven, had five-and-a-half bathrooms and five bedrooms. Besides the driveway and the garage, I could see, from the edge of the driveway, a martini deck outside the master bedroom, an outdoor hot tub, a rock waterfall, and a set of lush gardens that had been woven around the property.

I rang the doorbell and waited. I looked down at my right hand, which held the roses against my side. The footsteps that approached the door were heavy, which made me think that Tracey's father was a large man. It was just the shoes. Glen Simpson was a short, skinny man. His darting, probing eyes looked as if they were plotting something behind his glasses.

He was forty-four years old on that night, which made him slightly older than Tracey and I were in 2015.

His hair was brown, not at all blond, and he actually reminded me more of Michael, the corporate version of Michael I saw in 2015, than Tracey, who looked nothing like her father, except for their narrow waists.

"Hi," I said to him, and then I excitedly held up the roses, which caused him to back away. "I'm Ryan. I'm here to pick up Tracey."

With a faint nod, he permitted me inside, and then he turned away from me, letting the door swing open behind him.

☙❧

Tracey's house boasted dark hardwood floors, skylights, vaulted ceilings, and Tracey's father owned an impressive, valuable collection of West Coast artwork. Although these features gave me insight into the sensibilities and tastes of Tracey's parents, they revealed nothing to me about who Tracey Simpson was outside of Port Moody Senior Secondary.

I was left alone downstairs. I slipped off my shoes, my Reeboks, and tiptoed through the downstairs hallway, facing the living room entrance. The kitchen was on my right. It was dominated by a stainless steel island, which was encircled by lacquered cabinets. I wanted to immediately return to 2015, just to see if I could find the house again.

I was halfway between the kitchen and the living room entrance, when I saw the first sign of Tracey's presence in the house, staring straight ahead, at the puffy recliner in the living room. I pictured Tracey's flailing limbs extending over its beefy arms when she watched television after school, or when she was stuck at home with her family on a Saturday night, wishing she was elsewhere.

Then I heard Tracey pacing back and forth upstairs. The balls of her feet made a hollow impression, and I could almost hear her mother talking on the phone upstairs. But her voice was muffled by the sound of running water.

I was so preoccupied with what might've been going on with Tracey and her mother upstairs that I didn't notice Tracey's father, when he reappeared in the hallway. I thought he was going to invite me into the kitchen, or into the living room, but he instead pointed upstairs and sighed. "I'm sure she'll be right down," he told me, taking my measure as if he was looking at a spreadsheet.

"This is a nice house," I said.

"Where do you live?" he asked me, forgetting my name.

"I live in College Park," I said, pointing outside, upward.

"What are your plans next year?" he asked.

"Business," I said. "I'm on the business administration and commerce track."

I heard Tracey walk downstairs.

"That's great," he said, smiling, his voice jumping several octaves. "It sounds like you know what you want to do."

She was wearing beige dress pants, a gold belt, and a white blouse, with a little makeup and red lipstick, enough to accent her natural beauty without overwhelming it.

She stepped in front of me, eying the roses my limp fingers dangled in front of her. "Hi," she said, and then she took the roses from me. I watched her sniff one of them in the hallway.

Then Tracey's mother arrived downstairs.

When I looked at Tracey's mother in the hallway, I had my first glimpse of Tracey as a woman. Their features were nearly identical, most notably the doe eyes and silky blonde hair.

If I could've photographed Tracey, as she looked in her forties, alongside her mother that night, anyone who saw that picture, who didn't know them, would've thought that they were sisters. The same pattern would develop between Tracey and her daughters.

I'd made a labyrinth of Anmore on the way to Tracey's house, but it unraveled like one of my shoelaces on the way out. It was a really tiny area.

"My mom and I have started working on my prom dress," Tracey said as we left the cul-de-sac behind. I was reminded of the red dress she'd worn to the first prom, and of Chad Fletcher, and how much I wanted to erase both of them.

After leaving Anmore, I returned to downtown Port Moody, headed for Perry's, a restaurant that was perched on the corner of St. Johns, halfway between the downtown strip and the high school. The restaurant, which was converted into an office building, was named after Perry Roe, a successful businessman, who became Port Moody's first mayor in 1913. Perry's was his family home, built in 1910, and it was the grandest house in the city.

The former residence, which would come to be known as the Perry Roe Building, was, at a height of two-and-one-half stories, easily the tallest building on St. Johns. It was a lovely example of the foursquare style, with its axial floor plan, balanced facades, bell-cast hip roof, double-hung wooden sash, one-over-one windows, projecting second floor corner window bays, symmetrical detailing. I didn't think Tracey noticed any of that.

On the night Tracey and I had dinner there to begin our first date, Perry's was still the family home where Perry and his wife, Wilhelmina, held glamorous gatherings for Port Moody's elite.

From the parking lot, we climbed a long staircase that led to a wraparound veranda. Then we approached the front entry door, facing painted thistles on beveled glass, which was an arresting tribute to Perry's Scottish ancestry.

The main dining area, like the rest of the house, had oak floors, wooden detailing, and there was also a fireplace, one of three in the house. There were two narrow columns of tables, and Tracey and I were seated against a wall, to the right of the window. We had a clear view of the mature trees out front and the back-and forth-traffic that whizzed past St. John the Apostle Anglican Church.

Even with the swooshing of the traffic, it was easy to be transported back in time, especially when meditating on the central staircase that winded its way up through the house. I wondered, before we were served, what it would've been like to be there in the 1920s, in the house and Port Moody, with Tracey.

"I've been here before," she said.

"This house is over a hundred years old," I said.

"There are so many old houses around here," Tracey said, pointing out the window. "Port Moody has so much history."

"It sure does," I said.

One day in 1946, a train pulled into Port Moody, carrying a payroll bag for the workers at the local mill. As was the routine, someone tossed the bag off the train, to be picked up by the postmaster. But the bag had been tossed so clumsily that instead of landing cleanly on the ground, it ended up on the railroad tracks.

There was at least $20,000 inside. When the train pulled away, it ripped the bag to shreds, sending the bills floating in its wake. When the millworkers realized what was happening, they scrambled to gather as many of the bills as they could, using their hats and pails. They did a great job, because less than fifty dollars was unaccounted for.

The dining area was three-quarters full, and I couldn't see anyone I recognized, until I looked at the busboy and saw that it was Kevin Barlow, the middle linebacker on the football team. He'd also been in English Lit with me and Tracey in the first semester. Kevin sat at the front of our row. I remembered everyone who was in that class.

Kevin rushed over to our table as soon as he saw me. After he filled our glasses with a pitcher of ice water, Kevin and Tracey nodded at each other, which concerned me. "Hey, Ryan," Kevin said, quickly turning his gaze over to Tracey.

"This is Tracey," I said, which I sensed was unnecessary.

"We're in Biology," Tracey said.

"Did you like that earthworm lab?" he asked her.

Tracey laughed. "That was crazy."

I wasn't happy. I reached for the menu. "What do you recommend?" I asked Kevin, trying to break their rhythm.

"The salmon's really good," he said, straightening the cutlery on our table. "Everyone loves the pepper steak."

After Moody, Kevin attended SFU, which was only the beginning of his post-secondary odyssey, which would take him to the University of Edinburgh, and then the Hague Academy of International Law in the Netherlands, and then the University of Windsor in Ontario. All of this finally culminated in a Doctorate of Laws in 2007.

He would go on to become a criminal defense lawyer in Vancouver. He specialized in defending child molesters and rapists, which sometimes put Kevin's name in the newspapers and his face on the evening news, for very bad reasons.

Kevin left our table when the waiter arrived. I ordered a Shirley Temple, and Tracey ordered mineral water. We both had salad. I asked for Thousand Island dressing, and she chose Catalina.

"Where are you going next year?" Tracey asked me.

I really thought I was going to see Tracey again in September 1991, back at Moody, in English Lit class.

"I'm going to Douglas," I said. "I'm more interested in you. Are you going to SFU, UBC?"

"I'm probably going to UBC," she said.

Between 1995 and 1996, when many of my classmates at Moody graduated from SFU and UBC, I checked the lists that were published in the *Tri-City News*, looking for Tracey. But I never saw her name.

"What courses are you going to take?" I asked.

"I'm going to take arts and science classes in the first semester," she said. "I haven't decided on a career yet."

"Neither have I," I said.

I ordered the filet mignon for the main course, while Tracey picked the roast beef. We both had boysenberry pie for dessert, with another Shirley Temple for me and tea for Tracey.

We started talking about music over dessert, and I lamented the quality of the music we were subjected to throughout high school. I was thinking about MC Hammer, Milli Vanilli, Rick Astley, Vanilla Ice, and Wilson Phillips.

"I like Depeche Mode," Tracey said.

I liked Depeche Mode too, and they were at their commercial and creative peak in 1991, after a slow, steady buildup throughout the eighties.

I mentioned the Smashing Pumpkins, by accident, nearly forgetting that their debut album, *Gish*, had been released in May 1991, just before graduation. "I never heard of them," Tracey said.

"*Gish*!" I said.

"*Gish*?" she asked, looking confused.

"Their first album," I said. "It just came out, just as we're graduating. They're great. They were great. We were left with MC Hammer, Deee-Lite, Rick Astley, and Wilson Phillips. How did we survive? Why couldn't Nirvana have released *Nevermind* six months earlier?"

Tracey nodded in recognition. "One of the guys in the smoke pit has a Nirvana tape," she said. "He says they're awesome."

"It must be *Bleach*," I said, "their first album. How did you end up in the smoke pit? You don't look like a smoker."

"My friends hang out there." she said.

"Alice in Chains and Jane's Addiction were great," I said. "They won't play any of their songs at the prom. They'll only play top forty, no exceptions. They'll give us Depeche Mode. They're played on MuchMusic and Zed around the clock."

"They're definitely top forty," Tracey said.

"Who else was there?" I asked.

"I used to like the New Kids," she confessed.

I had a dark secret of my own. "I loved the B-52's," I told her, "and my friends laughed at me."

I had loved the Cure throughout my teens and still listened to those songs. "High" was my ultimate Tracey song, followed closely by Madonna's "Cherish." Those songs perfectly embodied the interchangeably sad, whimsical sides of unrequited love.

"Maybe it wasn't such a bad time after all," Tracey said.

I remembered Concrete Blonde and Midnight Oil. "There was some good stuff," I admitted.

☙❧

Our conversation turned to the unlikely subject of dirt bikes as we walked to the car.

On the only day I recalled Tracey being absent from Math class, Mr. Phillips revealed to us that Tracey was at a race.

"How'd you get into riding dirt bikes?" I asked her.

"My brother Todd," she said.

"I remember you missed class one day," I said. "I never would've guessed that you would ride dirt bikes."

"It's fun," she said. "It can also be dangerous, but I love it."

"I'd love to watch you ride sometime."

"We might go to the track on Sunday," she said.

I assumed that she was referring to one of the trails around Eagle Mountain, but there were BMX and Moto-cross tracks scattered all over British Columbia. Throughout the nineties, I used to check the local race results, looking for her.

I took Tracey's left hand and led her to the passenger door. I maintained my grip on her hand as I opened the door for her. I didn't let go until she was seated.

"How about we go see a movie?" I asked Tracey in the car.

"Okay," she said, nodding. "Which one do you want to see?"

I reached into the backseat and removed the entertainment section from the Friday edition of the *Vancouver Sun* newspaper, which I'd bought at the Shell station.

There were three movie theaters located within the Tri-

Cities region—Coquitlam, Port Coquitlam, Port Moody, as well as Anmore and its neighboring municipality, the village of Belcarra—in 1991. They all died. They were betrayed then murdered.

The Coquitlam 4 multiplex was demolished, and the site was taken over by a Best Buy store. Eagle Ridge Cinemas, which was located one block east of the Ioco Road turnoff, was converted into a health club. The theater inside Lougheed Mall, which was located one block west of the Burquitlam Funeral Home, was replaced by a sporting goods store and a travel agency.

I loved them dearly. But I didn't want to see them again.

The front page of the movie section was dominated by large ads for the films *Backdraft* and *City Slickers*, while *Hudson Hawk* and *Only the Lonely* were clearly on their last legs. Their ads had been trimmed, and the theaters were abandoning them like rats leaving a sinking ship.

I turned to the back pages, looking for the art house, cult, and independent titles. I found ads for the films *Eraserhead*, *The Gods Must be Crazy*, *Henry: Portrait of a Serial Killer*, *Last House on the Left*, *Metropolitan*, and *The Rocky Horror Picture Show*. I saw the small ad for *Truly, Madly, Deeply* at the bottom of the last page. It was playing at the Oasis, a theater in downtown Vancouver.

"Let's go see *Truly, Madly, Deeply*," I said, showing the ad to Tracey.

"What's it about?" she asked, staring at the title.

Truly, Madly, Deeply was about a woman who was grief-stricken over the death of her lover, who returned as a ghost. He tried to push her to move on with her life by tarnishing her memories of him. At the end of the film, he stood by and watched as she began a new life with another man.

"Did you like *Ghost*?" I asked her.

"Yes," she said enthusiastically.

"Then you'll love this," I said. "It's *Ghost* with brains."

I drove out of the lot and turned left onto St. Johns, headed for the Barnet Highway.

Because of photography, I'd gotten to know Vancouver almost as well as Port Moody. As Tracey and I entered downtown Vancouver, I was able to compare the before and after scenes, the mental snapshots, of Vancouver's skyline. This revealed the extent, the actual cost, of Vancouver's development since the night Tracey and I went downtown. The Oasis theater building Tracey and I visited that night was, in 2015, just one of over 600 skyscrapers in the city.

After leaving the parking garage, Tracey and I had to walk along two rundown streets to get to the Oasis, which had a neon sign. The sign leaned over the sidewalk. All of the letters flickered, except for the A, which moodily glimmered in dribs and drabs, conserving its energy. *Truly, Madly, Deeply* shared the marquee that night with *Rosalie Goes Shopping* and *Santa Sangre.*

When Tracey and I arrived at the box office window, we were met by the owner, an enthusiastic but clearly exhausted man who could've been in his late-forties or early-sixties. Through the window, I saw his heavily pierced, tattooed daughter standing behind him.

Besides their daughter, the owner and his wife were supported in running the theater only by the teenage usher, a boy, who ripped our tickets in half, and a bald man with the ravages of AIDS, who functioned as a cinema repairman and janitor.

There were no pictures in the lobby of Fred Astaire, Jack Benny, Sarah Bernhardt, the Marx Brothers, Mark Twain, or any of the other greats who'd performed there. When they'd appeared on stage there, the Oasis, which opened in 1891, had alabaster handrails, a copper marquee, Corinthian columns, polished brass doors topped with intricate stained glass windows, and two enormous chandeliers, which hung down from the atmospheric style ceiling. Again, I don't think Tracey was interested.

The owner's wife was behind the concession counter. She was tending to the erratic popcorn machine when Tracey and I approached the counter.

"Hi," the woman said, wiping the steam and sweat off her forehead with the back of her left arm. Then she waved her left hand over the counter like a magician. "Welcome to the Oasis."

"It's such a beautiful theater," I said. "I wish there were

more of these places, these cinematic cathedrals, around."

"Tell that to the city council," she said.

I looked down at the candy. Without consulting Tracey, I reached down and picked up chocolate covered peanuts and Reese's Peanut Butter Bups for myself, Jujubes and Red Twizzlers for her.

Tracey and I were alone when we entered our movie theater. We were slightly closer together in our seats than we were in English Lit class, but our positions were reversed. Tracey sat on my right in the middle of the theater.

I turned sideways in my seat and faced her. "I never saw you last year," I said. "If we hadn't been in the same English Lit class, I probably never would've known about you. We weren't in junior high together. I went to Banting."

"I went to Moody Junior," she said.

"You were on the other side of the class the first time I saw you," I said, "and then one day you sat down next to me."

She nibbled off the ends of a Twizzler with her front teeth and used it as a straw when she sipped her orange Gatorade. "I wanted to sit next to you," she said.

"I remember everything about you," I said. "Your clothes, your hair, everything you said and did. You…uh…spoke to me twice. The first time you asked to borrow some paper. Then you asked me a question about *The Canterbury Tales*. You asked me about the miller."

"The miller?" she asked, looking genuinely puzzled.

"You asked me if that was the dude with the red beard, the black nostrils, and the wart on his nose," I said, hoping to jog her memory, trying to paint a picture with my hands. I saw a slight glimmer, but I thought she was being polite. "It blew me away to hear you say dude. I didn't have an answer for you. I hadn't read the book at all, because I couldn't concentrate on anything except you. I failed the class, and I almost didn't have enough credits to graduate."

We locked eyes. Then we both leaned forward. "I've never kissed a girl," I said, licking my lips. Then we kissed. We kissed again during the coming attractions trailers, and then she stared straight ahead at the screen until the movie was over.

I looked up at the balcony before the trailers started and spent the entire film meditating on the indivisible relationship between the dead and the living.

❧❧❧

Tracey exhibited no outward reaction as she watched the film but was bursting with excitement after we left the theater and returned to the street. "I loved that movie," she said.

"I'm glad," I said. "I wanted you to see it."

"Who was that actor who played the husband?" she asked as we headed back to the parking garage. "I think I've seen him before."

She was talking about Jamie, the man who reappeared as a ghost to Nina, his lover. The film never definitively stated that Jamie and Nina were married, and the point was irrelevant. "Alan Rickman," I said. "He was the villain in *Die Hard.*"

"It was heartbreaking," she said and then cleared her throat. "He was willing to let her be with another man, because he didn't want her to spend the rest of her life being lonely and sad."

We kissed again on the street. My right arm was around her neck, and I'd almost put her in a headlock when I pulled her into me for the kiss. "Could you do that?" I asked her. "Could you just let go of someone you loved like that? I don't know if I could do that. I actually think it's impossible."

"My grandma died when I was eight," she said. "I loved her so much. I couldn't do anything without thinking of her and breaking into tears. Then I felt this presence, like someone holding me, and I just knew that she was okay and that my being sad all the time would make her sad."

"Sometimes I think death is easier," I said. "When someone close to you dies, there's finality. You know you're never going to see and speak to them again. As time goes by, you get used to this. But when someone you love, someone you can't imagine a future without, goes away, simply disappears, it's like they're also dead, gone. But you know they're out in the world somewhere. It's that open-endedness that drives you crazy. Do you know what I mean?"

⋐⋑⋐⋑

Tracey's house was dark and still when I escorted her to the front door. "I had a great time," she said, reaching down deep into her pants for her house key. Her curved, sizable breasts were fully defined through her blouse.

"Do you want to go out tomorrow?" I asked her. Then I remembered that I was scheduled to work at the Petro-Can on Saturday.

"Where do you work?"

"The Petro-Can up at Burquitlam Plaza," I said, pointing in the general direction of Snake Hill. "Maybe we can do something tomorrow night."

"I'd like that," she said, her key brushing the face of the lock until it found the keyway. The key slid in and out of the lock three times before Tracey pushed it to the hilt, which stimulated the rotating joint and the shaft.

She did this so silently compared to the fireworks that erupted whenever I'd used my house key late at night. I'd tried to be that soft on prom night, when a taxi brought me home in the wee hours. But my key made a sharp crackling sound when I feathered it into the lock and turned it clockwise, loud enough to awaken all of College Park.

Before she entered the house, I wrapped my arms

around her waist and lifted her off her feet. "I love you," I said.

☙❧☙

Zed played Brighton Rock's "One More Try" and Kenny MacLean's "Don't Look Back" on the drive home, both of which were on my Tracey songs playlist. It was a quarter past midnight when I stepped through the front door.

On a typical Friday night, I would've gone down to the basement to watch the end of Johnny Carson and then waited to see David Letterman. Sometimes I stayed up for *Friday Night Videos*, which was as far as I could go.

I stood in the hallway and listened to Dad's snores, long enough for me to time the breaks. The snores got louder as I entered the living room and found Dad on the couch, his mouth open. He had yet to watch *Death Warrant* and *Ski Patrol*, which were inside the two cases that were by his side. *Narrow Margin*, *Predator 2*, and *Spaced Invaders*, all of which he had rewound and returned to their cases, were on the glass table. "Oh, Dad," I said to him, realizing that these were all one-night rentals.

I watched Dad sleep on the couch until I heard Mom's prolonged creak on the stairs. She barely looked at me when she entered the living room and initiated the process of getting Dad up to bed.

Before I left the living room, I looked over at the sliding glass door and the empty spot where Mom's bed was. The color of the night reminded me of when I used to stand in front of her bed, or out in the hallway, watching her sleep, listening for her breathing, which was uneven. Her lungs would hold her next breath captive for two, three seconds before she exhaled, so every breath sounded like it was going to be her last. I was afraid to go upstairs.

On the Friday before her death, Dad was driving Mom home from the hair salon, one of her rare outings, when she had a massive seizure in the car and briefly lost consciousness.

I was at a casino when this happened, trying to make a living as a poker player, which was like saying you wanted to become a professional crash test dummy or kamikaze pilot. Before Mom died, my gambling addiction forced me to sell the jewels of my comic book collection, which gutted me.

When I returned home on that Friday, I found Mom slumped in her chair. Her eyes were half open, and her speech was slurred and unintelligible. Her voice had been reduced almost to a whisper.

On Monday night, her last night, I stood over her bed before I went upstairs, looking down at her, trying to understand what she was telling me through her incoherent mumbling. Her breaths came in difficult, short gasps, and her eyes were frantic and knowing, confirming my worst fear.

I was awakened early the next morning by the sound of

Dad's voice downstairs. He was pleading with Mom, trying to revive her. When I ran downstairs, Dad was in the hallway with Mom, who was in her wheelchair. "Do you think I should call nine-one-one?" he asked me, looking and sounding discombobulated, all over the place.

"Call them!" I barked. "What are you waiting for?"

Instead of following Dad to the hospital, I went to the casino. It was just after three o'clock when I got off a bus in College Park, just down the hill from the driveway. I found Dad's car in its normal position, which I took to mean that Mom was resting comfortably in New Westminster, at Royal Columbian, the hospital she'd stayed at in 2000.

If not in the hospital, I willed Mom to be in the living room, on the bed or in her chair, as I unlocked the front door. I heard Dad sobbing when I entered the house and stared into the living room. I lowered my gaze from the sliding glass door and the sky, and the bed and Mom's chair, to Dad, who was in his chair. His head was darting back and forth between the television, which was on, and Mom's empty chair. "Your mother died this morning," he said.

"Okay," I said, turning toward the bottom of the stairs.

❧❧

I heard Mom leading Dad toward the stairs as I entered my room. I sat down on the end of the bed, in front of the dressers. Then I turned and stared at the yearbook drawer. I went back and forth with myself before I opened the drawer and removed the pristine copy of the 1991 yearbook, which was less than twenty-four hours old.

Tracey's voice started replaying itself in my mind. I tried to sort through everything she'd told me, everything new I'd learned about her.

The new 1991 yearbook was resting on my legs when I looked back down into the drawer and saw my old, tattered copy of the 1991 yearbook from 2015.

With both hands, one on each side of the old yearbook, I gently raised it out of the drawer. With the book still closed, I slid my right index finger along the outer edges of the pages until I found the fingernail-shaped crevice. When I touched it, I only had to flick the yearbook open. I looked down at the creased, scratched, yellowing page and saw her face.

Although I told myself that what I was seeing couldn't possibly be real, I sat there for at least an hour, staring into Tracey's face, her yearbook picture, waiting for her to say something.

Chapter 11

After reliving June 7, 1991, I reentered my forty-two-year-old body. I awoke on Friday, October 2, 2015, the day Dad's obituary was published in the *Tri-City News*. I was still in the bedroom when I opened my eyes. I was sitting on the end of the bed, facing the yearbook drawer. It was just before seven in the morning, and I couldn't remember waking up, getting dressed, showering, anything. The 1991 yearbook—my original, worn copy— was on my lap.

In terms of trying to explain what was happening to me, the first possibility I considered was that I'd experienced the same form of time travel through self-hypnosis that author Richard Matheson described in his classic 1975 science fiction novel *Bid Time Return*, which I'd always thought of as a fantasy romance.

There were some definite similarities between my quest and that of Matheson's protagonist, a dying thirty-six-year-old writer named Richard Collier. Like me, Collier saw the woman of his dreams, a famous stage actress from the nineteenth-century named Elise McKenna, in a picture. He traveled back in time to pursue a relationship with her.

But Collier fell in love with a woman from the 1890s, about a century before I discovered Tracey, and his ability to transport himself into the past depended almost entirely on his mind, while I only needed the yearbook. Collier's obsession with Elise McKenna was triggered by a single picture, while I had a handful of pictures of Tracey to choose from.

The worn yearbook on my lap wasn't open to Tracey's yearbook picture but to the color picture of her sitting in front of a row of lockers with Robin Daly and Shannon McKenzie, the lone color picture of Tracey in either of the Moody yearbooks.

Her lips were the color of cherries, her hair had been highlighted, and she was wearing a black leather jacket. The fingers on her left hand were curled around a five-dollar note, and her nails were red. The most striking feature of the picture was how cleanly and crisply the photographer had captured the moment, which gave the picture the aura of timelessness. It could've been taken yesterday.

After kissing Tracey, this became my favorite picture of her.

When I was transported into, or through, the color picture, which was the only way I could describe the experience of being able to inhabit a picture just before it was captured, I found myself standing in a downstairs hallway at school, about twenty feet away from Tracey's locker.

I immediately looked around the hallway for the student with the camera.

Yuri Semenuk was the yearbook photographer in grade twelve, and we were lucky to have him, although we didn't know it at the time. He was a great photographer.

When I found him on the downstairs floor, he was standing in front of a row of lockers, blocking my view of Tracey. I ran down the hall to where Yuri was standing and examined his camera, which was a low end Kodak. Then I stepped forward to take a closer look at Tracey, who was, once again, sitting in front of the row of rainbow-colored lockers with Robin Daly and Shannon McKenzie. This was only seconds before the picture was taken, and it was obvious that the three of them were blissfully unaware of Yuri, the camera, and certainly me.

I was able to move back and forth between the bedroom and the hallway. In the bedroom, I drilled my eyes into her face and the page.

In the hallway, I leaned down in front of Tracey until I was inches away from her face and the black Hugo Boss sweater she was wearing in the picture. As I peered through the holes in her slightly torn jeans, I badly wanted to kiss her. But I was completely invisible to her and everyone else in the hallway.

Looking down at the picture, I waved my right hand over her eyes and face, and then I rubbed her lips on the page with my fingers.

Then Yuri took the picture. I closed the yearbook and lifted myself off the bed.

After I left the bedroom, I entered the computer room with my laptop. When I opened the laptop, I quickly discovered that my absence, from Langley and my studio, had gone virtually unnoticed. My only remaining professional obligation was a wedding, which would turn out to be my final act as a photographer.

The only messages I received were from Allison Williams, my attractive, much younger assistant. She asked if I was okay and gently inquired as to when I'd be returning.

I didn't know what to do about Allison, her light blue eyes, and incandescent red hair.

On that day, in June 2014, when I spotted Laura Hartley, the girl who'd reminded me of Tracey, while photographing a high school graduating class, I felt Allison's eyes on me as we were driving back to my studio. When I turned and looked at Allison, who was twenty-seven years old at the time, she was trembling with emotion, smiling but ready to burst into tears.

"Why don't we go to my place later?" she asked me. "I'll make dinner."

"I have to work on some photos," I said.

Her bottom lip started to quiver. Then she reached out and touched my right shoulder with her left hand, which she immediately withdrew when she saw my horrified reaction. "I love you," she said. "Do you want to be with me?"

"I'm too old," I said. "It's too late for me."

Before I left the computer room, I emailed her and told her I'd be returning in a few days, a week at the most, which was a promise I couldn't keep.

Then I searched for Tracey online. But I had no more success than before.

ဆၠဆၠ

It was quarter to eight when I left College Park and drove down Snake Hill toward Anmore.

On my way to Anmore, I made an impulsive decision to stop off at Moody Middle School, formerly Moody Junior High.

I'd only been to the school once before. In the seventh grade, I, the best speller Seaview had to offer in 1986, went to the school with Dad one evening to represent Seaview in a regional spelling bee, which I exited very early.

Banting Middle School and Moody Middle School encompassed grades six through eight in 2015, compared to the eight-through-ten model that existed when I was at Banting Junior High and Tracey was at Moody Junior High. If the middle school model had been in place when Tracey and I were teenagers, we would've entered senior high school in September 1987 instead of September 1989. I could've had four years with her.

Although I arrived at Moody Middle School before any students were there, I very much felt like an intruder, and I was gripped by self-loathing as I got out of my car and looked around.

Pulling myself together, I entered the school office, where I saw a woman, the receptionist, sorting the morning announcement pages on the front counter.

"Good morning," I said, already losing my breath. "Sorry to bother you. I was a student here back in the eighties. I'm looking for a yearbook. I lost mine in a fire."

"What year are you looking for?"

"I entered junior high in September 1986, so I left here in 1989," I said. "I'd like to see the 1989 yearbook, if that would be possible. I just want to look at some pictures and take down some names."

Although I'd worn a suit and tie and had grown a temporary beard, I could see that she no more believed that I was a fully-formed adult than I did. "That's a long time ago," she said. "You don't look that old."

"How old do I look?" I asked her, smiling but choking up.

"Thirty," she said. "Maybe you could be thirty-one, thirty-two."

"Do you have the yearbook here?" I asked, voice breaking. "I just need to see a picture."

"What's your name?" she asked.

"Tom Miller," I said.

Tom Miller, who went to Seaview, was an IT manager at BC Hydro in Vancouver. He had a wife and three children.

She reached for the phone on the counter and made a call. Then she pointed upstairs. "The librarian has it," she said. "She's waiting for you."

♋♋

The librarian refused to look me in the eye as she coolly handed me her copy of the 1989 yearbook, which was the only year I was prepared to ask for. After she turned away from me and walked into her office, I sat down at one of the tables, in the middle of the library, with the yearbook, which was in mint condition. When I opened the 1989 yearbook in the library and flipped through it, I recognized many faces and names from Moody Senior. I saw Morgan Bradbury and Chad Fletcher.

I slowed down when I reached the S names. I stopped on a page that ended with a girl named Peggy Shyer, who hadn't gone to Moody Senior. I turned the page and held it upright for a few seconds before I let it fall. Then I looked down at Tracey.

Beyond the effortless, natural smile, which was her most constant, enduring feature, her cheeks were softly rounded when the picture was taken, and her hair was shorter than I'd ever seen it before.

Yes, I was madly in love with Tracey Simpson in junior high.

I was still staring at the picture when a student, the first one I'd seen after I was inside the school, entered the library and dropped a book into the return slot.

I ripped out the page and returned the rest of the yearbook to the librarian. "Did you find what you were looking for?" she asked me.

ɞɞɞ

I had little difficulty finding Anmore and Tracey's street again on October 2, 2015. I'd been there. The cul-de-sac had added two houses since my last visit. I parked directly across the street from Tracey's former house, which had been heavily remodeled. I'd gotten out of my car and was approaching the house when a black Mercedes entered the cul-de-sac and pulled into the driveway. It was just after nine o'clock in the morning.

A man in his late twenties got out of the car and saw his wife in the doorway. She was cradling their baby in her arms. I was trapped halfway between my car and the man, facing the Mercedes, when she ran outside to greet him.

Then they looked at me.

&s010;

Against my better judgment, I returned to Moody Senior on October 5, 2015.

I went to the gym to watch a basketball game. Although I was excited to see the Port Moody Blues boys, who were ranked fifth in the province, I identified much more closely with their opponent, a faceless, nameless team that was completely overmatched. The discouraged players gave up very easily, which reminded me of my season.

The Moody Blues players on the floor that night were freakishly athletic, and they were tall. Our team was slow and vertically challenged. I was the second tallest player at six three, which meant that I was a backup center trapped in the body of a shooting guard.

The gym's retractable bleachers were three quarters full by the time the 2015 game started. I sat in the corner, toward the back of the school, supposedly a part of this fraternity of high school basketball players. But I knew I'd never really been a part of anything. I estimated that the sum of my playing time in grade twelve equaled two whole games.

I scored in the last game of our season, which took place in the Moody gym on a Saturday night. We were playing the Centennial Centaurs, and the game was attended by several Centennial students I'd gone to Banting and Seaview with.

In the dying moments of that game, which we'd miraculously led at halftime, I was on the right wing, alongside the bleachers, when I received the ball, which I blindly flung toward Centennial's basket.

The benchwarmer gods guided the ball in for me. Then I heard thunderous applause from the benches and the crowd, all of it derisive.

The highlight of my season and a large portion of the rest of my life occurred the night before at Terry Fox Secondary. Because Fox was so close to Moody, Coach didn't feel it was necessary to take the bus, so he instructed us to find our own way to the game.

After Michael, Stuart, and I arrived at the school in Michael's car, we walked, solemnly and respectfully, past the statue of Terry Fox, who'd played basketball when he was a student there, in the 1970s, when the school was called Port Coquitlam Secondary. This was several years before Terry attempted to run across Canada on one leg to raise money for cancer research. He died on June 28, 1981, exactly ten years before my prom night.

Centennial and Terry Fox, both of whom were perennial contenders in the deep, tough Fraser Valley league, were our rivals only because of their proximity to our school. Our season—which included only one road victory, which came against a junior high team—was an unmitigated disaster for the ages, even compared to the lousy team Michael and Stuart played on in grade eleven, even considering the staggeringly low expectations Mr. Rockwell set for us.

Coach idolized Fox's coach, the steely, venerable Mr. Van Os. But Coach lacked the fundamental coaching skills and pedigree to be on his level. Coach was really just a History and Social Studies teacher, which made him feel small. He punished us for this.

Most of our road games were over before we even stepped onto the court, and that Friday night game looked like it was going to be no exception. The Terry Fox Ravens had a thirty point lead over us in the second half, which was when Coach looked down the bench, at me, and said, as if he could see my future, "Go out there and have fun."

When I entered the game, I joined Michael in the backcourt. He brought the ball up the floor on that first offensive possession, and then he passed it to me when we crossed the center line. I took several dribbles, and then I canned a three-pointer from just beyond the top of the key. I made another three from the left wing. The third one came from the left corner.

I scored more points in that narrow stretch of garbage time than I had in all the previous games combined. I finished that game with fourteen points. My last points that night came after I received a pass in the paint and was raked across my right forearm while in the act of shooting. The foul sent me to the free throw line, which was a place I'd never been before, outside of the backyard at home and the Moody gym during school hours.

When I stepped behind the free throw line, I could feel and see that all of the players who were lined up along the sides of the restricted area were in complete sympathy with me, as was the referee, a butch young woman, who smiled at me before she whistled the play live and gave me the ball.

My first free throw attempt went straight in. The ball barely touched the net. My chest heaved with emotion during the second free throw attempt, which kissed the iron then dropped in. My outburst triggered a full blown rally, which trimmed Fox's lead down to nine points, forcing Mr. Van Os, who became very angry, to send his starters back into the game to restore order.

෫෨෫෨

When Tracey reentered my thoughts, I was alone in the gym. The Monday night game was over, and the bleachers and hoops had been retracted. I was on the court, standing underneath the auxiliary lights. When I left the gym, I walked down the long hallway on the library side of the upstairs floor. I turned right at the end of the hall, headed for the English Lit classroom.

It was black inside the classroom. The right side of the room was illuminated slightly by the streetlights on Albert

Street. I looked through the glass, at the two desks nearest to the door. I entered the classroom and looked down at the two desks, which had undoubtedly been replaced and repositioned countless times over the years. But there were still two empty seats.

I'd calculated that, from the first week of September to the middle of January in the first semester of grade twelve, Tracey sat beside me for roughly eighty days. With each block lasting approximately seventy-five minutes, we might've been together for 100 hours.

I sat down in the desk that was directly in front of the door, my former position. I saw Tracey out of the corner of my left eye. I felt her beside me, on my left, against the wall.

I couldn't look at her in the class. I'd keep my head down; I'd turn to Aaron Lockwood, the redhead on my right; or I'd stare ahead at Mrs. Chambers, hanging on her every word but unable to process anything.

"Can I borrow some paper?" I heard Tracey ask me.

I turned to my left. She was looking at me. I nodded and excitedly reached into my binder. I grabbed a fistful of paper, which I hurriedly gave to her. Then I turned away.

"Thank you," she said. "The miller in *Canterbury Tales*," I heard her say to me as my back was turned to her. "Is that the dude with the red beard?"

"Yes," I said, staring at the window. "He's the dude with the red beard, the black nostrils, and the wart on his nose. He was big and strong, and he was a great wrestler. He told the story about the clerk who slept with the carpenter's wife."

I slowly turned to face her.

Chapter 12

I awoke to an empty, silent house on June 8, 1991, the morning after my first date with Tracey. Before my eyes completely opened, and I looked around the bedroom and out the window, I was worried, lying face down under the covers, until I turned on the radio and heard *Casey's Top 40*. It would've been impossible to construct the beginning of a typical Saturday morning in June 1991, or at any other point in my Banting and Moody years, without including Casey Kasem's voice.

I listened to a segment of the program, sitting on the edge of the bed, facing the door. Before I entered the bathroom and took a shower, I moved over to the window and stared in the general direction of Anmore and Tracey's house.

The one-night video rentals from Rogers Video were gone when I came downstairs, along with the BMW and Brad's Jeep Wrangler. I heard the dryer running in the basement.

It was early in the drying cycle, which told me that my parents were somewhere between the Rogers Video store, which was located halfway between the Burquitlam Funeral Home and Lougheed Mall, and the Save-On Foods supermarket in Coquitlam, three blocks east of the Ioco Road turnoff.

Before I finally separated from College Park and Port Moody, and adolescence, these were the boundaries of my world, the farthest points I needed or wanted to reach.

I went down to the basement with my breakfast, a bowl of Fruit Loops and a cup of grape Crush, anxious to revisit Saturday morning television.

When I turned on the television, I saw Corey Haim in a rerun of *Roomies*, the short-lived 1987 sitcom Corey starred in, which NBC inexplicably placed on their Saturday morning schedule in 1991.

Corey was the defining teen idol of my high school years, from Banting to Moody and—although Corey's career in Hollywood effectively ended in 1989 with the release of the film *Dream a Little Dream*, Corey's last studio feature—he was ubiquitous to me throughout grade twelve.

On the night I scored my first points in a high school basketball game, he was waiting for me down in the base-

ment when I returned home—when I turned on the television, high as a kite, and watched the final scenes of the
1986 film *Lucas*, which contained Corey's best performance. His performance in that film was so honest and
touching that it suggested he was destined for greatness.

License to Drive, the 1988 comedy film in which he
played a teen who was desperate to obtain his driver's license so he could date his dream girl, was shown on television, on the Fox network, in the fall of 1990. I was still sitting beside Tracey in English Lit class when the film aired
that night, and my grip on reality was as tenuous as Corey's
place in history.

Corey, who would die in 2010, was most remembered
for the film *The Lost Boys*, the 1987 teen vampire thriller,
which I first saw at the Eagle Ridge in the summer of 1987.
Throughout my twenties and thirties, it seemed like the film
was shown on television at least three times a week, which
wasn't much of an exaggeration. It became an old friend.

It was on the television schedule for June 8, 1991. It
was being shown on CBS, and I would've watched it that
night, alone in the basement, if I wasn't going out with
Tracey.

When the *Roomies* episode ended, I entered the laundry
room and opened the dryer door. I found my Petro-Canada
shirt. After putting on my uniform, I sat in the kitchen and
looked out the window. I waited for my brother, Michael
and Stuart, my parents—any of them—to come back to me.

৩৯৫৩

The Petro-Can lived on an island within Burquitlam Plaza. We were pinned against the sidewalk, facing the back and forth traffic, which left us exposed and vulnerable. There were two rows of pumps, three pumps apiece, and there was a small convenience store. We rotated the full service chores, but we found that the most effective combination was when I pumped, Michael checked the oil, and Stuart washed the windows.

I loved manipulating the nozzle again. Muscle memory took over as I watched the numbers roll by. My right index and thumb were joined as I tapped the trigger, whenever I was close to the final total, and I was able to hit double zeroes every time. I never went a penny over.

I looked around the plaza, which was buzzing again. The stores formed a semi-circle around us, left to right, beginning with a Royal Bank branch, ending at the Shoppers Drug Mart. We were closest to the Dairy Queen, which was a sanctuary for us on a muggy afternoon.

The first regular customer I encountered that day was a woman in her late thirties, who batted her fake eyelashes at me when I appeared in front of her. Whenever she stopped by, I hoped to see her credit card, so I could find out her name. But she always paid cash.

"That'll be twenty dollars, ma'am," I said, weakly extending the right palm she liked to scratch with her talon-like nails.

She chuckled then reached for a silk purse. When she

did this, her plump breasts abused the red leather band trying to restrain them. It was not a fair fight. "That's so cute,"
she said. "Do I look that old?"

"Not at all," I said. "You're really hot."

She handed me a crisp twenty-dollar note. Her nails
brushed my palm as I pulled my hand away. When my fingers rubbed against the twenty, I felt the five-dollar note
stuck underneath it. I held it up to her. "You boys get some
ice cream," she said then drove away.

When she was gone, Michael held up a damp squeegee
and sprayed me and Stuart. Stuart and I grabbed our own
squeegees and retaliated, dousing Michael. We stopped
what we were doing when we heard the jingle of the store
bell. We turned and watched our boss, Vince Shaughnessy,
walk out of the store with an armful of firewood.

Vince was the kind of boss who understood that an
eight-hour shift at a full-service gas station was too much
for anyone, especially a teenager, especially on a weekend.
That's why he gave us five and six-hour shifts. He didn't
want lifers.

He was a bone-white, lantern-jawed British expat, who
always wore a Liverpool Football Club shirt under his Petro-Can uniform. I called him Sloth, after the character from
the film *The Goonies*. This was because of Vince's teeth,
which were, when I worked for him, in much worse shape
than mine were in 2015.

He was like an uncle to us. He always approached us in

a collegial manner, especially when we screwed up. He looked at the three of us on his way to the edge of the store, where he tossed the wood onto the existing pile. "Am I going to be stuck with you three bozos this summer?" he asked us.

"You can count on it," I said, looking at Michael and Stuart. "We'll be together one more year."

An extended lull in the traffic allowed the three of us to walk leisurely over to the Dairy Queen at the same time, which had never happened before.

We sat outside, on the bench, facing the Shoppers Drug Mart, waiting for the resumption of traffic, which was so nonexistent that we could've played touch football on the road.

I turned, to my right, and stared openly at Michael and Stuart, both of whom ignored me. Michael was methodically scraping the bottom of his *Dennis the Menace* sundae cup with his plastic red spoon, gathering as much of the residual fudge as he could, before he tossed the cup into the garbage can. When he sat back down, he turned and looked at me—rather he looked past me, through me, as if I wasn't there. I got chills.

Stuart's left arm slowly dropped onto my right shoulder. "We should get back," he said.

Michael and I nodded. As soon as the three of us got up off the bench, which we did in complete unison, the traffic returned. When I looked over at the station, there were two cars waiting for us. I told Michael and Stuart to return to the station ahead of me.

Then I ran over to a payphone and called Tracey.

๛๛

I picked Tracey up at six and took her to a party at Rex Heglund's house, which was in Eagle Ridge. Tracey opened her wallet in the car and showed me her driver's license picture. It was almost identical to her grade eleven picture, which was taken in the school cafeteria. "Do you remembering getting your driver's license," I asked her, staring at the license, noting her date of birth and middle name.

"I took my test with Hitler," she moaned.

I didn't get my driver's license until the fall of 1990, which put me behind almost everyone at Moody Senior, a pattern that continued throughout the rest of my life. I failed the knowledge test for my learner's license twice, which I assumed was unheard of.

I overcomplicated the test. When I stood in front of the touch screen in the driver licensing office, all of the answers to the multiple choice questions made sense to me, and my panic level escalated with every wrong answer, knowing that I needed sixteen correct answers out of twenty to pass.

After barely clearing that hurdle, my parents took every precaution to make sure I was ready for the driver's exam. They enrolled me in the Bestway Driving School, which was located in a small room across the street from Burquit-lam Plaza. The classroom portion was taught by a hairy, tat-too-covered biker, who looked and sounded very odd as he extolled the benefits of defensive driving and obeying the speed limit.

"Speeding doesn't work," he told the small group of us. "When you stay at fifty, you just make every green light."

Dad rented a Toyota Camry one weekend for me to practice with, and we drove around College Park and Gle-nayre together. We practiced the parallel parking in the Westhill parking lot one Saturday morning.

My Bestway driving instructor, a bearish guy in his late twenties, displayed a mordant sense of humor when he cri-tiqued my driving habits, and his left hand rarely let go of the brake during our nighttime drives.

Everyone at school had taken their road test at the driv-er licensing office on North Road, west of Burquitlam Plaza and Lougheed Mall, and they all mentioned the same noto-rious examiner who'd put them through hell, a man they'd collectively nicknamed Hitler.

My instructor was intimately familiar with Hitler, and he didn't want me to go anywhere near the North Road of-fice. "I don't think you're ready for Hitler," he told me. "You need to go somewhere else."

For my road test, he took me all the way out to the airy, flat city of Pitt Meadows, east of Coquitlam and Port Moody. He knew a female examiner in the Pitt Meadows office, and he felt good about my chances of passing with her. He took me out there one afternoon on a school day.

After I successfully parallel parked, on a neglected hill that could've accommodated a 747, the examiner told me I'd passed.

"Thank you," I said, placing my right hand on her left shoulder, which freaked her out.

"Don't touch me," she snapped, pushing my hand away.

"I didn't get Hitler," I told Tracey.

"You're lucky," she said.

⁓⁓⁓

Rex's parties could fill every inch of his three-story house, but there were no more than twenty-five people outside on the front lawn with me and Tracey at any moment that night, and everyone seemed to be in a contemplative mood, not inclined to conversation.

"You have a lot of friends," Tracey said, pointing at the crowd, most of whom I'd known since Seaview. Michael and Stuart were nearby.

"Not really," I said to her. "It just looks that way. But most of us were together a long time."

"I'm originally from Lethbridge," she said. "I had a lot of friends there, but we've lost touch. We moved here in '87."

"Lethbridge!" I said. "You're an Alberta girl! Wow. I'm a big Oilers fan."

"I know," she said, referring to the many days I'd worn my Edmonton Oilers hockey jersey to school.

I took her inside.

We sat down on the largest of the three couches in Rex's living room, facing a rectangular coffee table on which I saw a copy of the 1991 yearbook. I opened it to Tracey's headshot and pointed at her inscription. "'Cheers to the Class of 1991,'" I began, looking at her as I read along. "'Tracey will remember those just passing through, but a special few will remain forever golden. Thanks to amazing parents for everything. Gallant spirits can never be defeated.'"

"The gallant spirits line was taken from a quote by Wallis Simpson, the American divorcee who married King Edward VIII in 1937, after he'd abdicated his throne for her," Tracey told me. "There's a distant family connection."

"Who are the special few?" I asked her.

"My friends," she said.

I kept looking at Tracey's inscription, certain that I'd missed something over the years. "Who's passing through?" I asked her.

"You were."

∾

After we left Rex's party, we went roller skating at the

Ioco Recreation Center. Michael and Stuart followed behind Tracey and me as we approached the front of the building, which would become the Port Moody Recreation Complex.

I found it very complex when I went back there in 2015 and tried to get through the circuitous, multi-purpose facility. I'd gotten lost between the Olympic size ice rink and a smaller skating surface when I heard footsteps behind me. When I turned, I saw a burly man in a City of Port Moody costume. He looked at me as if I was a stranger, as if I didn't belong anywhere inside Port Moody. "Are you lost?" he asked me.

That's when I knew that the outsiders had completely peeled away and swallowed my hometown.

There was nothing complex about the Ioco Recreation Center in 1991, which was only a rink, with a single sheet of ice, and a lobby with a circular corridor and a few vending machines.

"What would you be doing tonight if you weren't with me?" I asked Tracey.

"Probably studying for finals," she said.

"Before that," I persisted. "Pretend that this is an ordinary Saturday night. Pretend you don't know I exist."

"I'd either be watching TV, or doing something with my friends," she said.

"Have you ever been roller skating?" I asked her.

"My Band class went roller skating in junior high," she said.

"What did you play?"

"I played the flute."

"I played the bass clarinet," I said. "Did you ever see anyone playing a bass clarinet? Do you even know what it looks like?"

"I don't think so," she said.

"Everyone else picked the clarinet, the flute, trumpet, and I picked that ugly monster, which I had to lug around for three years. The long case was too heavy for me to carry home, and the points always banged into my knees. It was a nightmare."

"Maybe you just wanted to be original, to stand apart," she offered.

"No," I said, with absolute certainty. "I never wanted to be original, stand apart, to be a misfit, nothing like that. My life just turned out that way."

After we laced up our roller skates, Tracey and I cautiously glided onto the polished floor, and then we slowly made our way around the rink. When we were no longer close enough to the guardrail to grab onto it and hold on for dear life, I skated behind her and supported her. Our fingers were locked together as if she were in labor.

At around eleven, three teenagers, two boys and a girl, calmly skated out onto the shiny, slippery surface and started handing out numbered sticky cards. They were wearing the black-and-white striped shirts worn by sports referees, which signaled the arrival of that night's contest.

That night's contest was held under rocket balls rules. Rocket ball was based on dodge ball. The so-called referees brought out a dozen or so Nerf balls, to be used by the skaters, following the stoppage of the music, to throw at other skaters to knock them out of the competition.

Skaters were disqualified if they got caught skating against the traffic—or for falling down. That was what happened to Tracey and me immediately after the last song I heard inside the rink that night, which was Olivia Newton-John's "Magic," ended.

After making sure that Tracey was all right, I looked up and saw a referee. He was a freckled teenager with big ears. After he smilingly ejected us with his right thumb, he ripped away our cards from my chest and Tracey's back.

As the referees gathered the balls for the next round, I saw that Michael and Stuart, who waved at me, had survived. The music had restarted by the time Tracey and I found surer footing on the rubber flooring.

After Tracey and I returned our skates, we followed the circular corridor to the building's back door, where I looked out at a soccer field, which was surrounded by a forest and railway tracks. My friends and I spent part of our summers on that field in the eighties, between 1982 and 1984, when our parents enrolled us in summer soccer camp, which was just a way for them to get rid of us for two weeks.

I reached for her hands. "Do you remember the first time I spoke to you, in the parking lot?" I asked her. "Of course you do. I'm getting a bit confused. Never mind. I wish I'd done that a long time ago. I think my life would've turned out very differently if I had."

"I'm glad you asked me out," she said.

I saw myself at school, upstairs, between the gym and the weight room, standing in the side hallway. My back was against a wall of lockers when Tracey appeared, by way of the long hallway. She walked right past me, on her way to the exit and the upper parking lot.

"I was standing in the side hallway upstairs, outside the gym," I said. "I was talking to someone, and then you appeared. You entered the hallway. I just stood there, frozen. I lowered my head as you went by me, as if I was your servant. You walked through the hall and went out the door."

"I don't remember that," she said.

I kissed her then backed away. I rubbed my hands over my eyes and face, expecting to wipe away tears. But the skin was as coarse and dry as sandpaper. "No," I said. "There's no way you could."

"Are you all right?" she asked, frowning slightly.

Before we left the corridor, I rested my head against hers with my arms around her, as if I could prevent the rest of her life from happening.

As if anything that happened between us mattered.

Chapter 13

I was awakened on Sunday morning by the laughter and muffled voices of my brother and father. I rolled over in bed, toward the window, and listened to them attempting to play basketball in the backyard.

I was about as good a high school basketball player as I was a photographer, but, as I still reminded myself, I was a better player than almost everyone at school outside of my teammates, and I was an all-star in the backyard, relative to the competition.

The backyard rim was ten feet above the ground and sat on the edge of a brick patio, just out of reach of the surrounding grass. The bricks were crooked and full of dead spots, which caused the ball to bounce in unexpected directions, making it hard to dribble.

"Here's the basketball player," Dad said, passing me the ball as I walked across the patio.

"Benchwarmer," Brad quipped.

I dribbled several times and made my first shot, a jumper, from about fifteen feet away, which was roughly the distance from the patio chairs to the hoop. "Compared to you, he's James Worthy," Dad reminded him.

Brad flashed a teasing smile at me, and then he walked into the house. Dad took the ball and dribbled over the patio. I watched him for a few beats, and then I got right up in his face, smothering him.

Dad backed away, exhausted, panting. When he clutched his chest, I thought about the leaf blower.

"Dad," I said, steadying him. "Are you okay?"

"I'm fine," he said. "I thought I was in better shape." He pointed at the house. "Brad told Mom he was sent home from school," he said. "Mom freaked, but then everything cooled down. She's going to try and get him into real estate."

"You don't need a brain to be a real estate agent," I said. "I mean, let's be honest."

"He's just going to look at it and see if it's something he can do," Dad said. "There must be something he has a passion for."

After Mom introduced Brad to real estate, he worked hard. He studied the market and paid his dues with the apartments and strip mall squares. After graduating to houses, he became one of the top producers in the Tri-Cities within two years. His profile expanded in tandem with his midsection, and his bulging face, which was, at one time, plastered over every bus stop bench and shelter between College Park and Anmore.

"What about you?" Dad asked me.

My small hands struggled to maintain control of the ball as I dribbled over the bricks. I stopped and launched the ball, which went halfway down before rolling out. "I'm going to work next year," I said, "up at the plaza with the guys, and I'll take some classes at Douglas. I'll try business, which is what everyone takes when they really don't know what the hell it is they want to do with their life. I'll transfer up to SFU, and then I'm going to drop out."

"Just try," Dad said. "Don't give up. Look around. You'll find something that interests you, and it will take hold of you, I promise."

I tossed the basketball onto the grass. It didn't roll or skip. It planted and stopped. "Dad," I said. "I'm a photographer."

When I'd first mentioned my interest in photography to Dad in the late nineties, I'd received a nonplussed reaction from him, but in June 1991, out in the backyard, he seemed genuinely excited. "A photographer!" he exclaimed. "That's great."

"No, it's not," I said. "It's nothing. I'm sorry, Dad. I disappointed you and Mom, and I disappointed myself."

"You never mentioned photography," he mused, as if he hadn't heard what I'd just said. "I've never seen you with a camera."

I went inside and called Tracey. Then I called Michael and Stuart and told them that they would have to get along without me at the Petro-Can that afternoon.

ଔଔଔ

When Tracey and I arrived at Coquitlam Center Mall, three blocks east of the Ioco Road turnoff, in her brother's truck, I assumed it was a detour. I never would've thought that the BMX dirt track Tracey had mentioned over the phone could've been concealed within such a dense urban area. There was also a five-hectare manmade lake and a skateboard park.

Town Center Park, our destination, was located three blocks north of the mall, situated behind Town Center stadium, where Moody Senior's football team played their home games. As we pulled into the parking lot, I heard the grinding roar of bike engines.

For most of the day, I stood on the edge of the choppy track and watched Tracey absorb punishment every time she bobbed up and down on the oval's lumpy hills. She would coast in the air and then land hard on the floor, and she repeated this several times on every lap.

After about ten trips around the track, Tracey got off

her bike and walked over to me. I'd examined Tracey's bike as we left her house and saw that it was a 1990 S&M with an old school frame. "That's an S&M," I said, pointing at the bars. "They're hard to find."

When I saw her shocked expression, I barely managed to keep a straight face. "How did you know that?" she asked.

"Oh, I read *Dirt Bike*," I said.

"You read *Dirt Bike Magazine*?"

"Doesn't everyone?" I answered.

I'd worn jeans and a white shirt. I spent most of the day holding the spare helmet Tracey brought along for me to wear, which I knew, without having to try it on, wouldn't fit my head.

I felt and looked plain beside Tracey, who was adorned with ratchet boots, an armored chest protector, and a helmet. Todd, her brother, barely acknowledged me the entire day. I was as inconsequential to him as the rainbow trout in the park's stocked lake.

When Tracey briefly looked away from me, I tucked my shirt deeper into my jeans, trying to showcase the physique I'd spent most of grade twelve developing for her. But I was still only about 170 pounds. I was no match for the riders, most of whom were bulky and ripped.

"I heard you liked big, muscular guys," I said to Tracey, flexing my upper body, pointing at the riders.

"Who told you that?" she asked me.

I was told that by Lyle Harper, an aboriginal student who graduated from Moody Senior in 1991 because he failed to do so the year before. Lyle, who was a full two inches shorter than me but weighed well over 200 pounds, specifically mentioned football players when he described Tracey's type to me.

I first met Lyle in the weight room, where I spent most of my free time at school in grade twelve, outside of the cafeteria and gymnasium. I'd previously seen Tracey leave the gym with Lyle, Robin, and Shannon after one of the assemblies. The girls were laughing about something Lyle said to them as they entered the hallway, where Tracey left them and disappeared into the nearest stairwell.

The next time I saw Lyle in the weight room, I asked him if he knew Tracey. He flashed a cheesy grin and nodded. When I asked him if she had a boyfriend, he stifled the urge to laugh. Then he shook his head. Like the gruesome scene in the library, when Stuart took it upon himself to speak to Tracey on my behalf, I shuddered to think what Lyle told her in the smoke pit.

After revealing my interest in Tracey to Lyle, who liked to show off in front of me in the weight room, as if to illustrate just far I had to go to be worthy of someone like Tracey, I intensified my weight training. I also turned to steroids.

My fear of needles and the connotations associated with them led me to take tablets. I bought them from Billy

Heflin, a twenty-five-year-old senior who came to Moody Senior by way of the Canadian Navy. The tablets increased my strength literally overnight without damaging my liver or shrinking my testicles, as we'd been warned.

The month-long cycle added a solid ten pounds of muscle of my frame, which didn't help me in my fight with Darren Clayton and didn't bring me any closer to Tracey.

Tracey slid her ungloved left hand over my arms and then my chest and pectorals. "Not really," she said. "None of them ever asked me out."

"I'm sure they wanted to," I said. "Do you go to Fitness 2000?" I asked her.

"Yes," she said, wide-eyed. "Do you go there?"

Lyle told me that Tracey had a membership at Fitness 2000, an underground athletic club and gym near Lougheed Mall. In the summer of 1991, I got a membership there. I went there almost every morning I could that summer, and I thought I saw her there twice.

As we kissed on the edge of the track, I saw, out of the corner of my left eye, Todd watching us then turning away. Then I sat on Tracey's bike. "This feels great," I said to her, grabbing the handlebars.

When she got on the bike, behind me, I felt her belly and the curve of her hips. I let my fingers run down her long, sleek legs.

Chapter 14

On Tuesday, October 6, 2015, after having digested all of the information Tracey had given me in 1991, I called a private detective. His name was Leonard Birdwell.

When I did a Google search, I found a 1985 *Los Angeles Times* article, titled "Cupid's Detective," which spotlighted his proclivity for tracking down, and often reuniting, long-lost friends, loves, and relatives.

"It's like watching a movie, a real cliffhanger, and finding that there's no ending," he said in the article. "You have to know how the story turns out."

In the *Times* article, Birdwell recounted the story of John, a lovesick former marine, who'd fallen in love with his general's fifteen-year-old daughter, when John was stationed in Hawaii in the late fifties. John got married and had children, but he couldn't stop thinking about the girl. Birdwell was able to find her, and he brokered a long-delayed reunion, which began with a phone call and ended in their marriage.

Birdwell once had a thriving business in Los Angeles, with employees and national media exposure, which made me curious as to how he'd ended up in Vancouver, alone, in a cramped office, in a building riddled with cracks and mold.

When I called his number, he answered almost immediately. "Birdwell," he said, after he cleared his throat of cigarette smoke and whatever he'd been drinking.

"I'm l—looking for s—someone," I said, already stammering. "It's a girl I went to high school with. I just want to know what happened to her. I'm not a criminal or an ex-husband, nothing like that. Honestly, I don't know how to describe myself."

"Calm down," he said, in a cavernous, gravelly voice. "Why don't you come to my office, and we'll talk about it, face to face, okay?"

മ⁊⁊

Birdwell's building was located on Bute Street in downtown Vancouver, in the West End. Bute was close to Davie Street, which was known as the prostitution capital of

Canada. The ten-story building, which was half commercial and half residential, looked like a badly maintained apartment building from the outside. Birdwell's door—*Birdwell* appeared above *Confidential*—sat at the far end of the fifth floor, facing the back of the building, next to an acupuncturist, who was away on an extended vacation, and the janitor's closet.

Birdwell was a gruff-looking, whiskery man in his early sixties, who reminded me of Ricky Jay, the great character actor and magician. He looked at me like I was the first potential client to have walked through his door in years, a notion I discounted when I saw the stuffed filing cabinet behind his desk.

The *Times* article was framed on the wall, along with several other articles, accreditation certificates, and letters. I couldn't see a computer or a laptop in the office. The lone shelf in the office functioned as a museum to his glory days back in the seventies and eighties and the methods he'd once relied on. I saw a black landline telephone in the closet and a stack of phonebooks covering North America.

I didn't see a live phone in the office until he received a call just after I'd sat down in front of him in a slightly unbalanced wooden chair. As he pulled the ringing phone out of his pants, he showed me the picture of Tracey I'd emailed him the previous morning.

I'd sent him Tracey's 1991 yearbook headshot, along with all of the information about her that I believed to be true, based on what she'd told me. But Birdwell already possessed the skeletal details of Tracey's life before I arrived.

I had the 1991 yearbook with me.

"I can't believe I'm doing this," I said, shifting around in the chair. I'm sure he'd heard that a million times before, but he seemed happy to be hearing it again instead of dealing with the divorce and surveillance cases that were his bedrock as of 2015. It was obvious that he hadn't played cupid in a long time and missed it.

"Relax," he said, tapping the phone, again summoning Tracey's face to the screen. "Just tell me what you want."

I took a deep breath and sat upright. "There's this girl I had a crush on in high school," I said, pointing at the phone. "I can't stop thinking about her. I'm not a stalker. I don't want to talk to her, write to her. I don't want to disrupt her life in any way. I just want to find out what happened to her. I want to know who she is now. I have to know."

"It's the curiosity, isn't it?" he asked me. "I used to do a lot of high school sweethearts, until Facebook came along."

"A crush," I said, tossing the word on the floor and staring at it. "I never spoke to her, never asked her out. She wouldn't even know who I am. I don't want her to know I'm looking for her."

"Did you try Classmates, Facebook, any of those sites?" he asked, saying their names as if they were his mortal enemies.

I was terrified that Birdwell would search the Class of 1991 Facebook page himself in order to find Tracey, and I wanted none of that. I made myself crystal clear to him on that point. "She's not on Classmates, Facebook, any of the reunion sites," I assured him.

"What about her friends?" he asked.

"I can't ask anyone," I said. "I haven't spoken to anyone from school in over twenty years. She truly doesn't know me. What the hell would I say?"

Although I'd sent Birdwell the yearbook image of Tracey, I wanted him to see what I saw, so I held up the 1991 yearbook and opened it to Tracey's headshot. I gently laid the yearbook down on the desk. It was my new copy of the 1991 yearbook, the one I'd purchased, for the second time, on June 7, 1991.

"I found out some things," I said, scribbling the date of birth and middle name I'd seen on Tracey's driver's license, along with her Anmore address, onto a piece of paper. "She lived there," I said, pointing at my impatient handwriting. "That's in Anmore, which is on the outskirts of Port Moody. I was there. I think she went to the University of British Columbia, but I'm not sure. I'm not sure about a lot of things."

Birdwell looked at Tracey's smiling face on the page as if he was a proud father on his daughter's wedding day. But when he looked at me, I saw bad news in his eyes. "What are you looking for?" he asked me.

"I just want to know what happened to her," I said.

He closed the yearbook and glared at me. "What are you looking for, Ryan?" he repeated. "What do you want from her now?"

"I want a picture," I said.

∽∾∽∾

When I entered Math class on Monday morning, on June 10, 1991, Tracey was already in her seat. I calmly walked over to the back right corner of the room and sat down directly in front of her, in Morgan Bradbury's vacated desk. As the start of class neared, I stared ahead at Chad Fletcher's empty desk. I never saw him again.

"He's going to give us our grades," Tracey said, her voice shivering as she pointed at Phillips's desk.

"Don't worry," I said. "You'll get an A."

"I don't know," she wavered.

I saw Phillips open his mark book. "I know," I said in a prophetic tone. "You'll get an eighty-nine."

When Phillips called her name, she smiled at me and then nervously walked up to his desk. As before, she stood directly to his left when he pointed down at the number beside her name. "Eighty-nine," I whispered, just before he mouthed the number to Tracey, who immediately blushed, just like the first time.

"Thank you," she whispered to him, again, and then she

walked back down the aisle toward me.

"Eighty-nine," she told me as she sat back down. "He gave me an A. How did you know?"

"I can see the future," I said.

"Ryan," Phillips called out, two names later.

"Good luck," Tracey said to me as I pulled myself out of my desk. I smiled at her and then stared gloomily ahead at Phillips. "Sixty-two," I murmured.

⸽⸾⸽

Tracey had Biology in second block. After I escorted her to the Biology room, which was down the hall from my locker, toward the gym, I went downstairs, where I found Yuri Semenuk, the yearbook photographer.

I saw him sitting at the end of the downstairs floor's only long hallway, which was the most isolated, remote place in the school. Although Yuri, whose nickname at Banting and Moody Senior was Semi Dick, looked like a shipwrecked man, I couldn't hide the fact that I was very jealous of him.

I walked over to Yuri, cautiously, until I stood over him. When he looked up and saw me, he backed away so fearfully and forcefully that the back of his head banged hard against the wall behind him. Then he curled into a fetal position. I backed up slightly and waved my right hand in the air. "It's okay," I said. "I'm not going to hurt you."

"What do you want?" he asked, his back sliding against the wall, as if he was trying to scratch himself.

"I just want to talk to you," I said, holding up the 1991 yearbook. "You worked on the yearbook."

"Lots of people helped me," he said, defensively. "Everyone in graphic design worked on it. If you're mad about your headshot, blame Jostens."

Yuri rose to his feet and tried to leave. I blocked him. "Relax," I said, smiling. "You're a great photographer. I just wanted to ask you some questions. We're just two photographers talking to each other."

As a photographer, I no more considered myself to be a colleague of Yuri's than he ever would have with the rest of us from the Class of 1991. After leaving Port Moody, Yuri would move to England, where he would become a highly successful fashion photographer. He'd photograph the world's most gorgeous, high-end models, one of whom would become his wife. He'd also direct several acclaimed commercials and music videos. I would become a third-rate wedding photographer.

Yuri would always be the yearbook photographer.

I was worried that Yuri thought I was being sarcastic when I mentioned being a photographer, but he seemed to find me credible, and he lowered his guard slightly. "I'm not a professional," he said. "I'm learning."

I opened the yearbook and turned to the color picture of Tracey. "I love this picture," I said, pointing at her cherry lips. "Were there any other pictures that didn't make it into the yearbook? Do you have anything else?"

He pointed down the hall. "The graphic design room," he said. "I took hundreds of pictures that never made it into the yearbook."

I followed Yuri into the graphic design room, which was full of art supplies, drafting tables, and Mac computers. Yuri pointed into the backroom, and then he looked at the teacher, whose bearded face was familiar to me only from the yearbooks, who nodded his permission. "I think we still have the extra photos," Yuri said to me as we entered the cramped space.

"I'd love to see them," I said.

"Are you really into photography?" he asked me, reaching up to the top shelf, toward a stack of binders.

"Sort of," I said. "I'm not as good as you."

Yuri pulled down a large binder. He looked inside and then nodded and handed it to me. I took it outside and laid it down on one of the tables, in the middle of the room, facing the window and the forest. Most of the pictures inside were crooked and innocuous and had wisely been excluded from the yearbook. I was surprised they hadn't already been thrown away. The first picture that caught my eye was a picture from one of our basketball games. In the picture, Michael had just taken a shot, while Stuart was in the offensive paint, fighting for position, for a potential offensive rebound, against a taller forward from the other team.

The outline of our bench was visible through the maze of bodies on the floor in this picture, and while I couldn't see my face, I recognized my skinny arms and legs, my Reeboks, and my socks, which were rolled down to my ankles.

I found Tracey in a Beach Bash picture.

The Beach Bash, which was an annual event for the students and teachers at Moody, took place in the last week of September. The picture I found Tracey in showed a group of Moody Senior students sitting, standing, and walking on White Pine Beach, which was located on the northern edge of Port Moody, about ten miles down Ioco Road.

My friends and I didn't attend Beach Bash in either year. We chose to enjoy the day off school, though I was sure that Michael and Stuart would've gone if they hadn't been burdened with the responsibility of looking after me. After finding the picture, I wish I'd been there.

The edge of the water appeared on the left side of the picture, and the surrounding forest was on the right edge, leaving the sand in the middle. I focused my eyes on the girl in the two-piece black bikini. A white caftan was covering her back and shoulders. Her right hand was clutching an object in the picture, which I couldn't identify.

Although the sunlight obscured most of the faces in the picture, I was ninety percent sure that it was Tracey. I removed the picture from the binder and turned to Yuri. "Okay if I take this?" I asked him.

"Sure," he said, glancing at the picture. "It's of no use to anyone."

Chapter 15

The second class picture was taken on Tuesday afternoon, on June 11, 1991, behind the school again. Before I left the school with the rest of the students, I was in the library, sitting at a table with Michael and Stuart, waiting for Tracey. There was a buzz around the library and throughout the halls that day, on account of the rush of college and university acceptance letters that were circulating. I received my Douglas College packet the following week. Michael had received his on Monday and had it with him in the library.

"I got into Douglas," Michael said, waving his acceptance letter in our faces.

The acceptance requirements for the various postsecondary institutions had been explained to us during an assembly by Mr. Rockwell, who warned us that we needed a solid B average, a 3.0 grade point average, to get into SFU or UBC, instead of the traditional C-plus benchmark I'd pinned all of my hopes on. When I heard that, I knew I was going to Douglas.

Getting into Douglas required nothing more than a high school diploma or, as many joked, a pulse. "You only have to be off a respirator to get into Douglas," Stuart cackled at Michael, who quickly put the letter away.

"I won't be there long," Michael vowed.

The way it worked, in theory, was that you did two years at Douglas, five classes each semester, and then three years at university, resulting in a five-year degree. Michael would spend two years at Douglas and then three years at UBC. When he graduated from UBC in 1996, I would have less than two years' worth of credits to my name. "You sure won't, Mikey," I promised him.

"Dougie Daycare," Stuart chortled.

"Don't worry," I said to Michael, seeing his corporate image explode through his teenage pores every other time I looked at him. "No one will ever know you went to Douglas, or here, except us. It'll be our secret. When you're looking down at us from your high office window in the skyscraper, it'll feel like it never happened, because you'll be someone else."

In 2000, Michael—his corporate name would be Michael S. Gillies, CFA—would move to New York and join

Goldman Sachs as an analyst, covering pharmaceutical stocks. In 2009, he would be promoted to Vice President of Global Investment Research at Goldman, which had thousands of vice presidents. Michael would leave Goldman Sachs in 2013 and move to RBC Capital Markets, where he'd serve as managing director—Michael S. Gillies, MD— and oversee the firm's healthcare division.

He'd sit on the board of directors of several healthcare-related companies, play golf at Winged Foot, and he'd sometimes write articles for *Forbes*. For his 2011 wedding, to an Iranian-American cancer researcher, Michael would rent a beach resort in Mexico. He'd choose one of his UBC classmates to be his best man.

I saw Michael in 2013, on television. I was flipping through the channels and stumbled upon him. He was on the Business News Network, BNN, discussing drug stocks and making predictions. If I hadn't seen his name on the screen, I don't think I would've known it was him.

His eyes, which once sparkled with rascally intent, had become cautious, and the playful smile had turned prim. The wavy brown hair had blackened. His hair was lying flat on his bed, surmounted by the two protruding bones on his forehead.

He had, like me, turned forty, and we hadn't spoken in over fifteen years.

In 2015, Michael and his family, his wife and two sons, would live in a gorgeous apartment on Manhattan's Upper

East Side, in a co-op building where the cheapest unit cost $4.6 million.

In 2014, Stuart would be promoted to the position of General Manager at Electronic Arts Canada, the video game developer. In 2015, Stuart and his wife would have their fourth child, their first daughter.

The first time I saw Stuart's two oldest sons, through pictures, they were chubby tykes, spitting images of their father. But Stuart's firstborn son, Griffin, would enter the tenth grade in 2015, and the youngest of Stuart's three boys, Aidan, would turn six, the same age Stuart and I were when we entered Seaview.

When Tracey entered the library on June 11, 1991, before we left the school for the class picture, I saw her before she saw me. I rose from the table and met her halfway between the table and the door. Through the door and the window wall, we could see a growing crowd of students, all of whom were leaving the school.

"It's time," I said.

❧❧

When the Class of 1991 reunited behind the school for the second class picture, the collection of our bodies once again filled a rectangle between the grassy slope, which ran down from the edge of the grass field, and the pavement.

The Port Moody Senior Secondary Class of 1991

would distinguish itself, overall, in many ways. When I last visited the Class of 1991 Facebook page, I found 252 of my classmates, which left 144 members unaccounted for. Eleven of them were dead by 2015, which seemed like a disturbingly high number.

Besides Rex Heglund, I didn't recognize most of the names on the list of the deceased, and their faces triggered few memories when I looked at their headshots in the Moody yearbooks. There was no reason for me to believe, after nearly a quarter of a century of living in seclusion, that the news of my passing would've been received any differently. Besides Tracey, this was what motivated me to keep going.

"Did you know that Ryan Tremblay is dead?"
"I grew up with him. I'm sorry to hear that."
"He killed himself."
"I think I remember him."

The camera was resting comfortably on the tripod when we arrived outside. The photographer adjusted the lens several times then stepped toward us. He framed us with his hands as if we were starring in a movie he was directing.

"Is everyone here?" he asked, looking for hidden faces, studying our shape.

I stood directly behind Tracey, pressed against her, hugging her waist, my head on her shoulders, alternating between them. When I looked up, the photographer appeared ready to take the picture at any moment but then stopped and looked up at the white sky, waiting for the sun to break through, which it never did.

I saw Darren Clayton.

He'd stood behind me in the first picture, staring at the back of my head. But in the second picture, he stood at the far right edge of the picture, toward the forest, one row down from me.

After getting his bachelor of science, in biochemistry, from SFU In 1997, Darren would start working at a biotech company in Vancouver. He'd rise to the title of development operations manager by 2007, when the company would go bankrupt.

I was thrilled when I'd read that. However, the job market for biotech specialist always seemed robust, and to make matters worse, the bastard got an MBA from SFU in 2004.

I was forty-two years old in 2015. I had no education, no work history, and no plausible explanation for my disappearance.

When I looked away from Darren, I saw Robin Daly and Shannon McKenzie push through the crowd until they flanked Tracey. Whenever I needed proof of Tracey's existence, I searched for Robin and Shannon, both of whom were easy to monitor over the years, especially Robin, who was a member of every social networking service ever created. Both were married with children. Robin was a middle school teacher, and Shannon worked at the BC Wildlife Federation, where she was communications manager. I saw pictures of them.

When the indescribable moment the photographer had been waiting for, which I sensed, finally made its presence known to him, he took a picture. He took five more pictures, and then he gave us a thumbs-up sign, as I would have.

Then we all went our separate ways again.

Chapter 16

On Wednesday, June 12, 1991, after fourth block, Tracey and I went to her house and took each other's virginity.

Her house felt like our house to me as we stepped inside and took off our shoes. She took my right hand with her left and pulled me toward the stairwell.

"Do you have a camera?" I asked her as we moved upstairs.

When we reached the top of the stairs, Tracey let go of me and entered her father's study. She returned with a Canon Rebel camera, a fine camera for that time period, which I was able to handle with little difficulty. I snapped pictures of her all the way down the hall toward her bedroom.

I continued to snap pictures of her as we entered her

room. I lowered the camera when she fell backward onto the bed and stared up at me, unsmiling. Then I hovered over her with the camera, which she took from me and tossed to the floor. Then she took her clothes off.

She grabbed my left wrist and pulled me down onto the bed. I took off my shirt, and then I removed my pants and underwear. My erection, which I'd felt the entire day, thrust forward. It was longer than I'd ever seen it.

There was a direct correlation between the size of my hands and penis. My hands measured seven inches from top to bottom, which made them very small for my height, and my penis measured five and a half inches when fully erect. It shriveled to a garden slug, a one-inch nub, when I'd go limp. When I joined her on the bed, we were lying side by side, facing each other.

"My parents used to keep a pack of Trojans in their bedroom," she said. "I found them once when I was looking through their drawers. My mother's probably too old to get pregnant now. I wonder if they're still there. I don't think they do it much anymore."

"I can't get you pregnant," I stated. "We can do anything."

We started kissing. My lips moved down to her neck then her breasts. I circled the firming nipples with my fingers and tongue, feeling the jutting points, skimming the outermost tips with my front teeth.

She placed her right hand on the back of my neck and

guided me down her body, toward her rigid legs, which I spread apart. With the bottom of my right palm touching her pubic bone, I prodded the inner lips with my fingers then slipped my tongue through the opening. I gently pulled back the hood of her clitoris until it was exposed then licked the stringy appendage. Her bitter juices coated my lips and teeth then trickled down my throat.

At the moment of my climax, I was behind her, staring at her arched hips and wiry spine, leaning upward, as if I was attempting a sit up. But I was unable to rise more than a few inches off of the bed before I collapsed.

ოოო

We fell asleep.

Tracey lay on top of me, breathing hot air against my chest and neck, drooling on me. I packed a full night's sleep into two hours, which was my normal sleep pattern after Mom had her stroke, before I got married.

I dreamed that it was a Sunday morning. I embraced Tracey's snoring and waited for the patter of little feet to build outside our bedroom door.

I was awakened by Tracey slapping my arms. "My Dad is home," she said.

I looked up and saw Tracey standing over me, still naked, putting on her panties. Then she reached down to the floor and picked up my stained underwear, which I took away from her before she could inspect it closely.

We listened to her father's movements downstairs. His footsteps seemed to die away between the kitchen and the living room. But then they moved toward and up the stairwell, the feet dragging slowly up the stairs, pausing on the upstairs landing. Then his steps approached Tracey's door.

I reached for my watch on Tracey's nightstand and saw that it was almost five-thirty. "He doesn't usually get home before quarter to six," Tracey said, excitement building in her voice. "He works downtown, and the traffic is really bad. It's the same with Mom."

At Tracey's suggestion, I pushed her nightstand against the door. The spent camera was sitting upright on the dresser nearest to the window, seemingly undamaged.

There was a double tap at the door.

"Tracey?" her father called.

Tracey and I stood in place, until we saw the doorknob move, which was when I put on my underwear and clothes and then tiptoed over to the closet, which was spacious enough to hold five of me. The closet floor was bare except for a broken doll with no eyes.

"Tracey?" he called again, sounding worried, pushing against the door.

"Hi, Dad," she answered. "I'm moving things around in here."

"There's a car outside," he said.

"Ryan's here," she said. "We were studying."

"Hello," I whispered.

He coughed and then stepped away from the door and moved down the hall. I heard the master bedroom door opening then closing.

Tracey slipped back into her clothes. I listened to her father enter the master bathroom. When he turned on the shower, I swallowed a clump of rot, which fell straight down into the pit of my stomach.

"I'll call you later," I said, dragging the nightstand away from the door.

"Why don't you stay for dinner?" she asked.

"I'm disgusting," I said, squeezing my stomach muscles. "I couldn't face your parents like this."

She opened the door and pointed out a second bathroom at the far end of the hall. "Let's take a shower," she said.

☙❧

I returned to Birdwell's office on Wednesday, October 21, 2015, exactly two weeks after our initial meeting.

"I think you'd be better off not knowing," he'd told me over the phone. "Although curiosity can kill you, so can the truth. In your case, I strongly recommend that you leave this girl where she is."

"I appreciate your concern," I'd said to him with evident sarcasm, "but I need to know the truth, no matter how much it hurts me. It can't get any worse. This has destroyed my life."

When I walked into his office and sat down in front of him, the somber look on his face frightened me. I thought Tracey was dead, a possibility I'd only briefly considered. "Did you find her?" I asked him.

He held up a bulging manila envelope and placed it between us on the desk. I stared at it, cautiously, afraid to touch it at first. "You can know everything, if you want," he said, "but you'll be sorry."

℘℘℘

That night, I sat in the living room, holding the envelope upright, intending to scan through the contents before I went to bed.

I was staring at Mom's portable bed when I finally tore a small hole in the envelope. This unleashed Tracey's life, which floated through the darkened living room, depicted mostly through photocopies.

Birdwell had done his job with coldblooded precision. At the front of the tome was a copy of Tracey's birth certificate, which stated that Tracey Leanne Simpson, seven pounds and two ounces, was born on May 11, 1973, at Chinook Hospital in Lethbridge, Alberta.

Unbeknownst to me, Tracey entered UBC in the fall of 1991. She received her master of architecture degree in 1999.

Her married name was Tracey Coreau. She was living in Toronto, where she ran her own boutique architectural firm, titled Coreau Custom Home Designs, which specialized in modern condominiums and houses.

Tracey hadn't mentioned any interest in architecture or design to me, and I hadn't seen any inclination toward this when I was in her bedroom, which contained no artwork by Tracey, no drawing materials, sketchbooks, no pictures of landscapes or structures. There were no signs.

I found this troubling at first. I wondered if everything I'd heard and seen from her during our brief time together was entirely my creation. Until I opened that envelope, my relationship with destiny had been unbreakable. I'd been raised with the myth that we were all the architects of our future—that we could make elaborate life plans and see them through to the end.

But Tracey's biography, like most people's, consisted of accident and happenstance, and it was knit together by the choices she'd made when faced with potentially life-altering choices. The more I learned about her adult life, the more I realized that living was about adapting, not steering.

Birdwell included Tracey's wedding announcement from 2003, when she married Eric Coreau, a hedge fund manager who controlled billions of dollars. He was two years older than Tracey, which was an insignificant point for them as adults but would've created an unbridgeable divide if they'd met as teenagers. Birdwell's research failed to tell me how and when they'd met. But I was able to un-cover some disturbing clues, between Port Moody and To-ronto, and Montreal, where Eric was born.

I found Tracey Coreau's Facebook page, which con-tained no mention of Port Moody. When I first visited Tracey's modest website, it contained only her contact in-formation and some pictures of the houses she'd designed since 2009, the year she left the Toronto firm she'd worked at for eight years and went into business for herself.

The first current picture I saw of Tracey was from a 2014 article in *Canadian Architect* magazine, written about a house in cottage country that Tracey designed. At the end of the article, there was a picture of a smiling Tracey, stand-ing in front of the house with her satisfied clients.

Her hair was pulled back in the picture, just like on those dark, gloomy days at school, during the first week of every month, when she experienced her period. Her doe eyes were accompanied in the picture by a measured gaze I'd never seen before, and her face was fuller than it used to be. Children and marriage had added a layer of flesh be-tween the bone and the skin.

I saw a picture of Tracey's two daughters on Eric's Fa-cebook page. Their names were Ava and Lily. Ava was eight and Lily was ten in the picture, which was taken in August 2015.

Eric, in the only picture of him that I found in the enve-lope, had receding sandy hair and wore glasses. He looked dumbstruck, clearly amazed, as any man should've been, at his good fortune.

After completing my first viewing of the materials, I crammed Tracey's life back into the envelope, and then I plodded upstairs and cried myself to sleep.

Chapter 17

On Thursday, June 13, 1991, after school, I went to get fitted for my prom tuxedo. I drove—by myself, not with Dad like before—out to Pinetree Village, an unenclosed shopping center in Coquitlam. Dad's BMW and Michael's Mustang were in the parking lot when I arrived.

The shopping center was less than a block away from the Coquitlam 4 multiplex, where my friends and I had gone to see *Aliens, Back to the Future, Fright Night, Ghostbusters, Howard the Duck,* and many other films. Some of the films we saw there had been remade, or were going to be, which made me feel very old.

The tuxedo store, which was situated in an L-shaped strip mall, would become Flying Wedge Pizza, and I knew that Godfather's Pizza, Magicuts, and Nuffy's Donuts would also be gone. But on June 13, 1991, my thick hair was becoming unmanageable, and I needed a ten-dollar clip job before graduation. I would ask them to take at least one inch off the back. I liked my hair short at the front but not quite spiked. I hated sideburns. Nothing had changed.

I would've loved to have been able to visit Godfather's that afternoon and order a humble pie, which I would eat with a glass of crushed ice and root beer. Then I would play tabletop *Galaga*.

If I'd gone into Nuffy's, I would've picked out four double chocolates, four honey glazes, and four powdered jelly donuts.

No visit to Pinetree Village was ever complete without entering Save-On Foods, which was around the corner from the tuxedo store. Save-On had a large book and magazine section, and they had a video rental section, hidden in the back of the vast supermarket, which offered seven movies for seven days for seven dollars.

But there was no time for any of that.

When I entered the tuxedo store, I joined Michael and Stuart in front of the Michael Jordan standee they were fawning over. Although I'd never worn a tuxedo to any of the weddings I'd photographed, it was obvious to me that the Michael Jordan tuxedo we desired on that June 1991 afternoon didn't stand apart from the rest of the styles featured in the store. It was only a tuxedo.

If Wayne Gretzky had been endorsing a tuxedo in 1991, I was sure we would've picked his version, but we had Michael Jordan on our minds, and he looked so debonair in the store. His smile alone was so inviting that it would've been hard to say no to him, even if he'd just been a nameless tuxedo model. The tailor, who had nearly finished with Michael and Stuart when I arrived, rushed over to me. "I want the Michael Jordan one," I said to him, pointing at the standee.

"Of course you do," he said, buzzing around me with his tape measure.

After we tried on our jackets for the first time, the three of us stood together in front of a circle mirror, arms around one another. It was one of the last moments of unanimity that passed between us.

Then Dad crept behind us. He put his hands around my shoulders and pinched my nerves. "My boy's graduating!" I heard him say to himself, his voice cracking. "Look at him."

Dad's overexcitement made me think about Mr. Zaza, Moody's acerbic Italian-Canadian accounting teacher and self-proclaimed soccer expert. I took Mr. Zaza's class both years and got a B in both classes, only because I broke Mr. Zaza's cardinal rule of accounting: I memorized the material instead of knowing it. I couldn't diagnose a balance sheet in 2015 to save my life.

I was a Part-Timer, which was the nickname that Mr. Zaza gave to the slackers who thought they could scrape through high school without punishment. "You're wasting your time here," he said to us. "You should enroll in truck driving school."

Mr. Zaza told us about a former Part-Timer, a very poor student, whose father, like Dad, thought that graduating from high school was equivalent to winning the Nobel Prize. "His father bought him a new sports car and placed an ad in the *Tri-City News*," Mr. Zaza told us. "I saw the father at the graduation ceremony. He had tears in his eyes. I felt obligated to tell him the truth, but I didn't have the heart. Do you want to know what his son is doing now? He's a roofer."

I found my high school diploma buried in the kitchen cabinet above the stove. It was a browned, shriveled particle, wedged into an envelope, fused with my birth certificate.

After our fitting was completed, the tailor took back the materials from us, and then Michael and Stuart walked out of the store without a word. I waited until they disappeared into the parking lot, and then I turned and faced Dad. His eyes were closed, and his mouth had been sewn shut.

When I touched him, sliding my right hand along his cold cheek, his eyes flew open—just as I'd expected when I'd looked down on him as he lay in the cremation casket.

Then his purplish, sealed lips smiled at me. His words spilled out of my mouth. "Don't worry about us. Get on with your life."

Chapter 18

T he last day of classes on Friday wasn't the last day at the school for any of us, with the week of final exams ahead, but it marked the end of more than a decade of order. On the previous morning of June 14, 1991, someone pulled a fire alarm when I was in Math class, which evacuated the school.

When all of the students were outside the school, on the patio outside the front entrance, I found myself standing on the higher ground with Michael and Stuart, glancing down at Tracey, who was with Robin and Shannon. While they made Tracey laugh with whatever they said to her, I pretended to talk to Michael and Stuart, looking at them but really using them for cover, even though Tracey and I were separated by ten yards and at least fifty other students.

She appeared sideways to me while we were outside, not unlike my first partial viewing of her in English Lit. She never turned the slightest bit in my direction, to her left, so I could see her entire face. When she wasn't facing Robin and Shannon, or the school, she looked down at the concrete. Neither of us moved from these positions until the alarm prank was resolved.

When we all reentered the school, it was as if an alien device had been unleashed throughout the school while we were outside, creating a miniature black hole that consumed our attachment to the school, and each other.

After twelve years, the frail bonds of forced confinement and peer pressure had disintegrated, and we were all back to zero again. Throughout the rest of that day, the seniors' lockers made death rattle sounds as they were closed. Until the day was over, the future for all of us extended only as far as the end of the upcoming summer, and the first September of the rest of our lives.

I returned to Math class, which wasn't necessary, except to see Tracey for the final time in the classroom and the school. Despite the fact that she'd already received her A in the class from Phillips, she was at her desk, head down, feverishly working on a sheet of geometry problems that Phillips had given out in the last week, as a formality.

My ears braced for another pulled fire alarm when Tracey and I were holding hands over our desks. But it didn't happen the second time.

We walked out of the class and left the school. We returned to Tracey's house and made love for the second time in her basement.

ↄঙↄ

That night, I took Tracey to White Pine Beach, the site of Beach Bash, where we saw everyone from Rex's party. From the parking lot, which was full when we arrived, we slid down two steep hills, arriving at the edge of the beach.

Except for the high voltage power lines hanging overhead, which were easy to ignore, it felt like we were in the middle of a forest. The nearby development and houses were camouflaged by a hill lined with pine trees, and the surrounding hiking trails, which were accessible from either side of the beach.

After Tracey and I found Michael, Stuart, and the others on the milky white sand, I looked up and down the beach for the exact spot where Tracey had been standing in the Beach Bash picture Yuri Semenuk gave me.

I'd brought the Beach Bash picture with me. I showed it to Tracey, pointing out her bikini, her hair, the white caftan, everything. "Is that you in the picture?" I asked her. "It looks like you."

"That's me," she confirmed.

"What's that in your hand?" I asked her, pointing at the mysterious object her right hand was holding in the picture.

"Sunscreen," she said.

☙❧

The shell of the Port Moody Public Library remained in place several years after the contents were shipped to Ioco, along with City Hall, in 1995, so it was only when I opened the hollow metal front door that I thought I might've been asleep. The library Tracey and I visited that night had been dead for twenty years.

The black-and-white stills of early Port Moody were behind the glass in the foyer. People were sitting down in the cramped aisles, on the bile orange carpeting, their legs crossed, driven to delirium by the library's otherworldly intelligence.

I rarely visited the library more than twice a month, and most of the books were outdated and ragged, packed onto the overgrown shelves, blocking the few windows. It was always night in the library, regardless of the time outside, and I was always alone when I was there, lost in another dimension of time.

The library had two floors and a chilly, secluded basement where the children's books were buried. The top floor, where the magazines and non-fiction books were kept, was easily the airiest, brightest section of the library, with two rows of study tables and a view of the dark, narrow alleyway that ran past the librarians' parking spaces and a shoe repair depot that operated out of a shack, swarmed by over-hanging brush.

I searched the fiction section downstairs until I found the novel *Endless Love*. It was the copy I'd stolen from the Ioco library in 1995, after I ripped away the barcode and cover then glided past the sensor checkpoint that was parked at the edge of the front counter in the new library.

The book, which I read twice from beginning to end be-tween 1995 and 2010, stayed in the basement with me for several years. Then I took it upstairs with me, to bed. I re-read the opening and closing paragraphs on an almost night-ly basis, projecting myself into David, the novel's protago-nist, and Tracey into Jade, the girl who drove him to de-struction and madness.

The 1981 film, which starred Brooke Shields as Jade, was completely unfaithful to the structure and themes of the book but was a masterpiece compared to the 2014 remake, which was a disgrace to mankind.

I saw the Brooke Shields version for the first time on a sweltering afternoon in the summer of 1989, in the shade of the darkened basement. The film made enough of an im-pression on me that I sought the book out in the Moody li-brary in grade eleven, early in the first semester, when I was still enthralled with the newness of a flexible class sched-ule, which gave me more free time than I could spend.

For that first encounter with the book, I'd sat down in one of the carrels and skimmed the pages, only looking for the good parts, which were described in graphic, unrestrained detail.

I didn't know where Tracey was at any point throughout grade eleven. It's quite plausible, given the study habits she exhibited in grade twelve, that she could've been in the library with me at the same time I found the book. She didn't exist then, and I'd always wonder, as David did in the book, how much faster and further my life would've progressed if she'd remained anonymous.

I showed the book to Tracey. It was a compact, thick hardcover, over 400 pages, and so, even with the sickly-sweet title on the cover, it couldn't be confused with the legion of paperback romances that filled the revolving bookstands. It was a substantial thing. I thought it was the greatest novel ever written.

"Have you heard of this?" I asked Tracey, flipping through the pages.

"No," she said, shaking her head. "Wait. I remember the song."

"Lionel Richie and Diana Ross," I said, hearing the song play in my head. "It was the theme song for the film adaptation. Did you see the movie? Brooke Shields played the girl. It's a tragic love story. Well, the book is."

"I think it's been on TV," she said.

"I'd much rather you read the book than see the movie," I said.

I glanced at the snow-haired librarian behind the front

counter. I didn't know her name. She looked like an Agnes, Bernice, Constance, Gertrude, Lorraine, Mildred.

She was brandishing the same air of vigilance I'd witnessed up close years earlier when she busted me trying to make off with a pile of *Dr. Seuss* books. She shared a psychic link with stolen library books and sensed their anguish like no other librarian in the world.

I guessed that she either died, or relocated, or retired before the Ioco library opened in 1995, because I didn't remember seeing her there. I never would've stolen so many books from the Ioco library if she had been there.

It wouldn't matter to her what library the offense had occurred in, because a book was a book, a thief was a thief, and book thieves had a high rate of recidivism, me being a prime example. While I was back home, in 2015, I found over a hundred stolen library books, in the basement and my bedroom, most of which I'd never even opened.

I held the book in front of Tracey and directed her eyes toward the first page and the opening paragraph. Then I turned to the last paragraph on the last page. Tracey read the paragraphs and then nodded enthusiastically. "It's good," she said. "It looks interesting."

"I really want you to read the whole thing," I said, sliding the book under my jacket, squeezing Tracey's right hand, looking over at the front counter.

I tried to act cool as we walked out, breathing normally, looking straight ahead. But the distance between the fiction section and the edge of the foyer, which measured no more than ten feet on the way in, was an ocean by the time we reached the checkout. I thought we were in the clear when my acute peripheral vision, looking to my left, saw the librarian processing a book as we attempted to walk past her.

But she stopped what she was doing and looked at me. There was hope in her eyes as Tracey and I walked past the counter, which turned into despairing grief when I reached the foyer wall with the book.

ↄ৵ↄ৵

Video Magic was across the street from the library, around the corner from an arcade, and Great Canadian Sports Cards, which was the only one of the three still there when I drove past the block in 2015.

The first VCR Dad brought home was the Beta machine he bought in 1982, and we were the last family in Port Moody to move to VHS. Dad stubbornly refused to give up on our first VCR and accept the inevitability of Beta's obsolescence. "Oh, but the picture quality and sound on Beta is much better than that of VHS," Dad insisted again and again, all the way to the bitter end.

The end came in 1989, when Video Magic and the rest of the video stores in the Tri-Cities dropped Beta, forcing Dad to buy a VHS machine. Until then, when I was limited to the segregated corner that was Video Magic's Beta section, the rest of the store was an undiscovered country, whose capital city was located in the horror section.

I tried to get a job at Video Magic in the summer of 1990. I met with a young woman in the store one evening. I thought it went very well, but I never heard from them.

When Tracey and I walked inside, we were met by one of my teammates, Mark Patterson, who was standing behind the counter. Mark was our six four starting center and Mr. Rockwell's pet project and whipping boy. One time during a game, after Mark committed a turnover, or missed a shot close to the basket, Rockwell turned to us on the bench and declared: "That kid has hands of stone."

Mark raised his bushy eyebrows at me as Tracey and I walked by the counter. "Mr. Tremblay," he said, his playful voice flattening out the last syllable.

In the first semester of grade twelve, after the start of basketball practices, Mark was nice enough to make a copy of the film *Total Recall* for me. For the team banquet, a lethargic affair that was held at the Keg Steakhouse in Coquitlam, each of us was tasked with buying a gift for a teammate of Mr. Rockwell's choosing. Mark, whose head was just as big as mine but whose hands were much larger, was assigned to me, and I already had my inspiration, recalling Rockwell's frustration with Mark's leaden touch around the basket.

I gave Mark a can of stickum, the gunk used by some basketball and football players to improve ball grip. He appreciated the humor intended, as I did when Dennis Wong, our five two backup point guard, referenced my paleness by giving me suntan lotion.

I decided to limit my search that night to teenage films.

Of all of the John Hughes films, most of which Tracey told me she'd seen, the one I most identified with, and the one I was sure that Tracey hadn't seen, was *Career Opportunities*, which had been released in March 1991. It was a critical and commercial flop.

The film's male lead was an aimless recent high school graduate, trapped in the hometown most of his contemporaries had abandoned, unable to get his act together. In the film, he took a job as an all-night janitor at the local Target store and ended up spending the night with a rich girl he'd had a crush on throughout school. She was played by Jennifer Connelly, who was the first woman I fell in love with after I stopped seeing Tracey.

I became completely infatuated with Jennifer Connelly, who was born in 1970, in my early twenties. I searched for microfilmed articles about her in the libraries at Douglas College and SFU, and I watched, and then re-watched, all of her films, some of which were very obscure and difficult to find.

By the end of the nineties, I'd lost interest in her and returned to Tracey.

Career Opportunities wasn't in the store.

The first title that caught my attention in the store was

Permanent Record, which was a devastating, overpowering teenage drama about a popular teenager's suicide. It was a hard film to sit through. I'd last seen the film, which was released in 1988, on television in 2012. I cried throughout that viewing, brought to tears by the passage of time. I reflected that the teenager who killed himself in the film would've then been in his forties, just like the friends he'd left behind.

I saw Corey Haim in the store. His face was on the cover of *Lucas,* a wonderful film about first love. He looked so happy, compared to the horrible years that followed. He was wearing a football uniform and glasses, and his sweet vulnerability radiated through the plastic. Gone were the impish eyes and spiked hair from the teen magazines. Gone was the lopsided grin I found annoying in *License to Drive* and *The Lost Boys*.

Peggy Sue Got Married wasn't, technically, a teenage film. The film's protagonist, played brilliantly by Kathleen Turner, was a forty-three-year-old woman who found herself transported back in time to her last year of high school in 1960. She was reunited with her dead parents, her friends, and the boyfriend she ended up marrying. She knew everything.

I wanted to take Tracey back and forward in time with me. I had the pictures from 2015 with me. I put *Peggy Sue Got Married* back on the shelf. I found the box for *Say Anything* in the comedy section. When I saw Lloyd and Diane, played by John Cusack and Ione Skye, on the cover, I imagined that they were still, in 1991 and 2015, in the early stages of falling in love with each other. Her head was thrown back in laughter on the cover. Lloyd was staring at her.

Say Anything was released in the spring of 1989, when I was still at Banting, before Tracey. I remember watching Roger Ebert and Gene Siskel rave about the film on their show, *Siskel & Ebert*, and their enthusiasm made me sit up and take notice. I wanted to see it then but missed out. I didn't see the film until it was shown on television, on the Fox network, in the fall of 1991, after Tracey.

The film opened with Lloyd and Diane's high school graduation ceremony, where Lloyd realized that his window of opportunity for getting to know Diane, who received a scholarship to study in England, was rapidly closing. But he called her and asked her out before she got away from him.

"This is the one," I said to Tracey, grabbing the hollow yellow case behind the box.

꽃꽃

I took the right turn halfway up Snake Hill and drove through the Woodlands and past the Evergreens. I pointed out Seaview to Tracey. "That's where I started," I said.

When Tracey and I entered the house, the hallway and living room were dark. The only source of light downstairs came from the kitchen, above the stove.

"This is a very nice house," she said.

"I like it," I said, hearing Mom's feet trudge down-stairs.

I held Tracey in place beside me until Mom's pink slippers reached the bottom of the stairs. But Mom barely batted an eyelash at the sight of us on her way into the kitchen. There was a touch of familiarity in the way that Mom smiled at Tracey, as if Tracey was the latest in a long line of girls I'd brought home, or maybe because Mom had seen her face before.

"This is Tracey," I said, proudly holding Tracey out in front of Mom, who moved toward us until the three of us formed an impromptu circle in the hall. When they shook hands, Mom held Tracey's right hand slightly longer than seemed natural.

"Hi," Tracey said. "It's nice to meet you."

"It's nice to meet you, Tracey," Mom said. "Make yourself at home."

I held up the video. "We're going downstairs," I said, "to watch a movie."

"Oh, Dad rented more movies," Mom said, pointing toward the living room.

"I know," I said, "and I'd rather not hear about them, and I'm sure neither would Tracey."

I guided Tracey to the basement door, looking back at Mom, who was standing in the hallway, blocking my view of the front door.

"She's beautiful," she mouthed to me, pointing upstairs. "You can take her upstairs if you want."

☙❧

I led Tracey down into the basement, where I carefully sat her down on the corduroy couch, facing the television and the sliding glass door, handling her as if she were made of the most brittle china.

After I inserted the cassette into the VCR, I sat down beside her on the couch, to the left of her. We kissed intermittently as the film opened, which continued through the high school graduation scene, in which Diane, the class valedictorian, delivered the valedictory speech, while Lloyd, who watched her dotingly throughout the speech, absorbed every word.

I waited and then alerted Tracey to the first crucial scene, when Lloyd, after the graduation ceremony, worked up the courage to call Diane and ask her out. He looked in a mirror and brushed his hair with his fingers before he completed the call, which was answered by her father.

"That was me," I said, pointing at the screen. "Except I had already spoken to you, in the parking lot at school, and you answered the phone when I called."

After Diane returned Lloyd's cold call and reluctantly agreed to go out with him, she looked inside her yearbook for Lloyd, whom she only vaguely remembered, and recoiled at the sight of him. This was the only moment in the film when I disliked her. "Did you ever look for me in the yearbooks?" I asked Tracey. "Did you ever think about me?"

Tracey nodded. "Of course."

Watching the film with Tracey in the basement, I felt my long relationship with the film, which had, by 2015, spanned nearly a quarter of a century, being condensed into 100 minutes of the film's running time. This was a sobering reminder of the accelerated, wildly implausible timeline that ruled my relationship with Tracey in 1991, which had, by that night, only reached its one week anniversary.

"Do you think they're still together?" Tracey asked me after the final scene, in which Lloyd and Diane were seated together on a plane, about to fly to England.

"The odds are against them," I said, reflecting on the career of John Cusack, who turned forty-nine in 2015, and that Ione Skye, who seemed poised for stardom after *Say Anything*, had, like Tracey, faded into obscurity.

"They should make a sequel," Tracey said. "I'd like to know what happened to them."

"There should never be a sequel," I stated flatly. "We're all better off not knowing."

It was one-seventeen when I rewound the cassette and returned it to its case, which I returned to Video Magic, through their slot, after I drove Tracey home.

Before we left the basement, we stood in front of the

sliding glass door, where the curtains were halfway open. We listened to the breeze of the traffic at the bottom of Port Moody and stared out into the backyard. "I should take you home now," I said, removing the tiebacks from the curtains, which I pulled closed.

Chapter 19

When I flew to Toronto to see Tracey in October 2015, it was the first time I'd been outside of British Columbia since my days as a flight attendant, a job I held from February 1997 until November 1999, when I received a layoff termination letter from Air Canada.

I bought my first camera, a single-lens reflex, in the summer of 1997, during a stopover in Barcelona, and I quickly fell in love with creating images, focusing mainly on landscapes and wildlife. Dad helped me get the job at Air Canada, through his connections. He thought, as I did initially, that the social interaction and work experience would be good for me. But photography, and my working environment, only increased my detachment and isolation.

The more I looked around, and the keener my sense of observation became, the more ugliness I saw. I was disgusted by the passengers, who asked the same questions over and over again and tended to drop at least fifty IQ points between Vancouver and Toronto, which was easily our most common route. Most of my co-workers were, like me, trying to escape something, or someone, back home.

Fasting throughout the six-hour flight was easy for me, knowing how the food was prepared and where it came from, and there was no way I was going to use the toilets, even if it meant wetting my pants.

When the refreshments were served, I saw Shirley, who was pushing the snack wagon out of the galley. Shirley was a mother hen figure when I worked at Air Canada, despite only being in her early thirties when I first met her. Whenever there was chaos on a flight, she was a calming influence, quick to offer a smile, and words of encouragement, at the right time. I'd continued to think of her as a friend.

I had an aisle seat, and when Shirley appeared beside me, standing on my right, I did everything possible to make her remember me. I looked her in the eye, and I smiled, for the first time in years, despite my teeth.

But she looked at me as if I was a stranger. "What can I get you to drink?" she asked me, in her same jolly voice.

I shook my head, and then I opened my laptop.

Tracey Coreau had a Picasa Web Albums account, which contained thirty-eight files in 2015, beginning with her wedding to Eric, followed by family pictures. I started with Tracey's bridal shower pictures. Tracey was wearing jeans and a skimpy singlet in these pictures, joined by three other women, none of whom I recognized.

Then I moved to the wedding rehearsal dinner pictures. Eric and Tracey were sitting alone at a table in most of these pictures, away from their family and friends, looking very much in love. I saw Tracey's mother but not her father in this file.

There were pictures of Eric and Tracey opening their wedding gifts, one of which was a monogrammed, personalized towel set.

Then I looked at the pictures of Ava and Lily, whom I thought of as the daughters Tracey and I never had together.

∽✺∽

I was in Terminal 1 at Pearson Airport, which had four punishing levels. The precipitous downward spiral pounded on my knees, reminding me of how I'd plummeted into middle age. I was disoriented and exhausted when I reached the taxi queue with my light suitcase. It was nearly four o'clock in the afternoon, Toronto time, and Tracey's office hours ended at six.

Before I entered a taxi, I sniffed the air like a bloodhound for her scent, inhaling the diesel exhaust and jet fuel fumes, wondering what Tracey was doing right then. I pictured her in her office, circling a model and looking over the plans for a house she was building. She was surrounded by her three adoring assistants, recent university grads, all women, whom Tracey assigned entry-level, small drafting tasks and mentored.

Tracey had to rely on design software, out of necessity, but she still made time for the lost art of pencil sketching. She was an artist. I saw, online, three of her paintings, all abstracts and untitled, which were displayed at the University of Toronto gallery. They looked like multicolored shades of static, and I didn't have a clue what she was trying to say with them, but it was obvious that she had talent.

ഇഈ

Pearson Airport and downtown Toronto were separated by an antiseptic, tortuous highway with dead grass on its median strip, which made the taxi ride to the hotel seem much longer than the forty minutes it took. It was like traveling through a tangled, unknowable maze, which obviously symbolized the pointlessness of my search for Tracey.

I stayed at the Drake Hotel, which was located on Queen Street West, in the heart of the city's gallery sector. There was a vibrant Goth scene and countless Raves and sex shops. Every other building in the art and design district was a bar, or a gallery, or a nightclub.

There was no meter inside the taxi, and although I'd

seen a tight image of the Drake when I'd booked my room, I didn't know where I was when the driver stopped and then pulled out a map and ruler, which he used to calculate the fare.

"Are you lost?" I asked him.

He pointed to his left. When I looked across the street, I saw the Drake through the flimsy overhead wires and rusty metal utility poles that cluttered the front of the three-story building, which stood in front of a streetcar line.

The Drake looked and sounded like a nightclub, with a café patio situated on the edge of the building. The Drake had functioned as a flophouse and a punk den in its previous incarnations before undergoing a complete renovation in the early 2000s. The hotel totaled nineteen rooms. The rooms were stuffed into the second and third floors, beneath the rooftop patio, practically intertwined with the upstairs lounge.

The entire lower level was devoted to Queen's artsy, bohemian pulse. There was a portable art exhibit, a bar that converted into a nightclub, and a dining room that was promoting a lobster dish, which my empty stomach was crying out for.

There were no elevators in the building, so after the front desk clerk handed me my key, and a bow-tied bag of candy popcorn, I headed for the stairs.

My room only chewed up 150 of the building's 8,000 square feet, which would've been ideal for me if Toronto had really been the clandestine mission I'd made it out to be, and the precautions I'd taken to conceal my identity, and my purpose, had been at all necessary.

I wanted to get in and out of Toronto. I arrived on Tuesday, October 27, 2015, and I flew back to Vancouver on Thursday. I left a sparse trail behind me. There was nothing that could connect me to Tracey and her family. But I posed no threat to anyone other than myself.

The room had been outfitted with custom millwork, a glass shower, hardwood flooring, original artwork, and a flat-screen television. The only flaw I detected was a small crack in the shower glass.

A stuffed doll with a hairy chest was waiting for me when I walked through the door. It was lying on the bed with a welcome card attached to its left foot. I thought it was also a gift, like the popcorn, until I brought it home with me and discovered that the hotel charged my credit card an extra ninety dollars.

After I ate the popcorn, which was all I ate the entire day, I watched some television, and then I settled down on the bed and fell asleep quickly.

❦❦❦

The following morning, I got up at exactly six-forty, my normal time. After showering, I decided to put on my lone Armani suit, which was typically reserved for weddings.

After I left the room, I ate breakfast out on the patio—a blueberry scone and waffles. While I was finishing my coffee, I stared at the streetcar line, which was less than ten yards away from my table.

I rode a streetcar for twenty minutes and then boarded a subway car. From the subway station, I walked more than a half kilometer to Tracey's office building, which was located on St. Clair Avenue West. By the time I arrived in front of the eight-story building, salty, sour sweat was dripping into my eyes and mouth.

The building's main tenant was the Starbucks on the ground floor. I entered the building and sat in the lobby until I stopped sweating. Then I ambled between the Starbucks and the street for nearly an hour, carrying a bottle of water and a pack of sugar cookies, trying to talk myself into going upstairs.

I was standing directly across the street from the building, and the Starbucks, when I took out my phone and called Tracey's office. The call was answered just before the third ring.

I heard a woman's voice, which I didn't recognize but was certain belonged to an educated, married, professional woman.

"Hi," she said, her tone gregarious, and completely unguarded, as if the only calls she ever received were from clients or family and friends. "This is Tracey," she added after my long silence.

"I have the wrong number," I said, looking up at the building, counting the floors. "I'm deeply sorry."

"Don't worry about it," she said before she ended the call.

I returned to the lobby. It was nearly eleven-thirty when I first looked in the direction of the lobby's three elevators. I took the middle one upstairs to the seventh floor.

The lobby directory had revealed to me that Tracey shared the seventh floor with a cancer society, a chiropractor, a dementia support network, a food safety association, and a human rights organization.

When the elevator, which was dirty, stopped and opened, I saw a vase sitting on top of a plain mahogany table. There was a cheap ostrich oil painting on the wall, which hung crookedly from one of its hooks.

When I stepped out of the elevator, the cancer society was on my right and was closed. I turned to the left and walked in a straight line, down the hall, past Tracey's door, facing the food safety office, which was also closed.

Tracey's glass door was emblazoned with red letters that spelled out her firm's name, Coreau Custom Home Designs, on four lines that were vertically stacked on top of one another. I walked to the end of the hall and grabbed a pamphlet from the vinyl pouch that was attached to the door of the food safety office. Then I walked past Tracey's office. I repeated this at least twenty times, and my boldness increased with every attempt.

I saw a small reception area with a desk and a phone, but there was no receptionist in sight. Beyond the reception area, there was a workspace with a table that looked big enough to accommodate large architectural models.

I heard footsteps coming from the back of Tracey's office. I stepped to my right, as if I was going back to the elevator, and I caught a fleeting glimpse of Tracey as she moved around the desk. Her back was turned to me.

She was wearing a black wool suit, and her silky blonde hair was combed flat. I stood beside the door until I heard one of the elevators open. I turned to my right and saw a thirtyish man in a courier's uniform walk out.

We looked at each other for a moment. I straightened up and feigned a hacking cough, and then I fumbled through my pockets and took out my phone. I held the pamphlet out in front of me as we walked past each other.

I was standing in front of the elevators when I heard Tracey's office door open. I immediately covered the right side of my face and then banged the elevator buttons with my left thumb. When an elevator finally became available, I dove inside. I stood against the back wall, with my arms outstretched, until the doors slowly closed.

I was resting in the lobby, sitting on a couch, trying to marshal the energy to return to the hotel, when I saw Eric. I knew I was looking at Tracey's husband but, like with everyone I'd studied only through pictures, there were a hundred little differences when I saw him in the flesh.

He was taller than I expected, based on the pictures I'd seen, and he had long fingers and hands. I think he could've palmed a basketball if he'd wanted to, but he didn't look like he had the sports gene. I didn't want to think about his sexual prowess.

The girls, Ava and Lily, were with him in the lobby. I wondered why they weren't in school, until I saw that it was twenty minutes past noon.

The pamphlet I'd taken from upstairs was a review of safe food handling practices. I scrutinized every paragraph in the lobby, evoking my behavior in English Lit class. I was praying that Eric and the girls would take the elevator upstairs. But it was obvious that they were waiting for Tracey to come down. A few minutes later, she walked out of the elevator.

She was wearing dark gray pants, and there was a white gauge knit shell underneath the wool suit. She was carrying an architectural bag. I watched her put on designer glasses.

With Tracey and her family less than ten feet away from me, I remained still until they turned to walk out of the building. Then I sprang off the couch and followed them.

When I was outside, I turned to my right and was able to catch a glimpse of Tracey and her family before they were engulfed by a crowd. Ava was on Eric's left, and Lily was holding Tracey's right hand.

I was twenty feet behind Tracey at first, a distance I maintained for nearly two blocks. I'd slowly begun to close the distance when I saw Eric point ahead at a street that was lined with bistros and specialty shops. I was less than fifteen feet behind Tracey when they stopped in front of a traffic light, facing their lunch destination.

I was less than ten feet behind Tracey when a crowd formed between us, blocking my view of her. When the crowd dispersed, Eric and the girls were gone. I saw Tracey, who was breathing heavily, her back still turned to me. She was still staring ahead at the traffic light, which stayed red.

I stepped toward her. We were less than five feet apart when she suddenly turned and looked at me with the same empty expression I'd seen in my nightmares.

∽∾∽

I'd planned to spend the entire night at the Drake, in my room, but couldn't follow through, not with Tracey living just over ten miles away.

An Uber driver picked me up in front of the hotel in a Dodge Caravan and took me to the outskirts of a bustling dog park. The park was surrounded by a baseball diamond, a playground, and a myriad of running and walking trails.

I entered Tracey's enclave, Lawrence Park, through one of the trails, following the route I'd diagrammed back in Port Moody.

Lawrence Park, which had been ranked as the wealthiest neighborhood in all of Canada, was home to many corporate executives, former politicians, and dignitaries, including Canada's first female astronaut.

I walked past a golf club, a hospital, and several private schools to get to Strathgowan Avenue, Tracey's street, where I was completely exposed, standing in the middle of the street. There were no bushes, no sidewalks, and there was no moon.

She was living in another cul-de-sac. This took me back to Anmore, which immediately became the Lawrence Park of the Tri-Cities. The house on Strathgowan had five bedrooms, six bathrooms—with a cabana, a home theater, a mudroom and sauna, a pool—and was built on a sunny south lot.

I learned this not from standing directly in front of the house, because of its rampant three-dimensionality, but from the former listing for the property, which Tracey and her husband bought in 2007 for $6.5 million.

There was a soft glow emanating from the house, upstairs. It was barely bright enough outside for me to be able to identify the gray-tone brick and the countless layers of arches, shingles, and windows. I took a picture of the house with my phone, and then I moved through Tracey's gate and toward the front door, which was when I heard, to my right, powerful footsteps.

The sound momentarily froze me in my tracks on the front steps of Tracey's house.

I backed away, and then I turned and saw a flashlight's

searching beam approaching from the cul-de-sac entrance.

The flashlight was attached to the right hand of a bulky, thick man in his late twenties, who was wearing a community watch badge. I pretended as if I'd just walked out the front door, lowering my head on my way out of the cul-de-sac. I nearly collided with him.

"This is a private, restricted neighborhood," he said, perfunctorily and sarcastically. "Who are you?"

"I know who lives there," I said, pointing at Tracey's house, putting my phone away, flexing my hands in front of my chest so he could clearly see all of my fingers. "Tracey. Tracey Coreau. I went to school with her. Do you know her and her husband?"

"You were a guest at their house tonight?" he asked, eyeballing me. He reached for his phone but quickly changed his mind.

"I was just leaving," I said. "I'll never do this again."

He nodded and moved out of my way. I waved at him then walked away, turning, taking a last look at Tracey's house, which was completely dark.

Was she in bed?

Was she asleep?

Chapter 20

In June 1991, I made a concerted effort to treat the week of final exams like any other week of school. I arrived at school with Tracey on Monday morning, even though I didn't have an exam that day. I spent the morning playing basketball in the gym, waiting for Tracey, who had a History exam.

With Journalism and Math out of the way, the only exams I had to take that week were for Creative Writing on Tuesday, which required me to write a 1,500 word short story, and then Social Studies with Mr. Rockwell on Thursday, which was also Tracey's last day.

The Social Studies exam contained questions about the Boer Wars, Canada's Prime Ministers, the Industrial Revolution, the Napoleonic Era, the Oka crisis, and Vietnam. I finished the exam before everyone else, and I was confident that I'd done very well. I wished I could've found out how well.

When I closed the exam booklet, I looked at Mr. Rockwell until he finally noticed me. He was reading an issue of *Sports Illustrated*. His sneakers were up on his desk, the soles facing me. His hair, which was black and immovable at Moody Senior, would become deathly white, and he would have a hunchback posture and shriveled features.

After our season ended, we all chipped in to buy Coach a present, a plaque, which we presented to him at the banquet. He insisted that we all sign it, which I did in his office one afternoon, with the engraving tool he provided. "Time goes by, and you forget people," he warned us at the banquet.

I turned to the sunny sky and the trees outside the window. I listened to cars leaving the school, footsteps from the hallway and the stairwell outside the door, lockers being cleaned out.

When I placed the exam on Mr. Rockwell's desk, he gave me the smile reserved for his players. But I knew he wouldn't remember me in 2015.

After the Social Studies exam, I entered the library, where I found Tracey in one of the carrels again, studying.

I moved behind her, silently. I watched over her for several beats before I finally announced my presence by placing my hands on her shoulders and then leaning down to kiss her neck

"Hi," she said, turning to face me.

"How many exams do you have left?" I asked.

"Just Biology," she said. "What about you?"

I looked through the window wall and scanned the upstairs floor, which was nearly empty. "I'm finished," I said.

☙❧

On Monday morning of graduation and prom week, the Class of 1991 gathered at the Vincent Massey Theater in New Westminster, where the graduation ceremony was held, for a brief orientation session.

I drove out there with Tracey, going past Douglas College on the steep uphill climb. As we drove past the sidewalk next to the campus, I pointed at the school and pronounced, "This is where I'm going."

When we arrived at the theater, it looked like an opening day of school from any year I could remember. Everyone was standing outside in packs, grouped in the order of the prom table seating arrangements, acting strong and talking big, looking scared.

I found Michael and Stuart, and Tracey found Robin and Shannon.

For the orientation session, we organized in alphabetical order inside one of the theater chambers and took roll call. It was over in less than ten minutes, and then the class of 1991 broke apart again.

Tracey and I went to my house.

❧❧❧

I arrived back in College Park two days before Halloween in 2015. I bought a surplus of candy from the London Drugs down at Lougheed Mall and unearthed the decorations and lights from the basement, vowing not to look at anymore pictures of Tracey.

It was hard for the kids and their parents to find me and the candy that night. First, they had to navigate the long walkway between the street and the front door, and then they had to look through the blinding glare of the overhead lights Dad installed just before his death.

At eight-thirty, I set the flabby bag of remaining candy down in the hall and turned off the lights. Then I went downstairs and stood in the middle of the basement, under the light from the exposed bulbs.

The next morning, before I left College Park and returned to Langley, I called Brad and gave him permission to sell the house.

❧❧❧

The last couple I photographed—the couple who were

in my studio when Brad told me that Dad had died—decided to get married at the University Golf Club, near the University of British Columbia, which was the bride and groom's alma mater, and Dad's, and Michael's, and Tracey's.

Allison was cold toward me before the wedding, and she refused to look at me during the ceremony and the reception, which I took to mean she was letting go of me.

As we were packing up to leave, I looked ahead to the rest of my life and saw myself remaining completely alone.

When I gave the pictures to her, she nodded, and then she turned away from me. I leapt forward and grabbed her right shoulder. When she turned around, startled, I kissed her.

Then we went to her apartment, where she relieved me of my virginity.

We were married less than six months later.

Chapter 21

On graduation night in 1991, we were spread throughout the rooms inside the theater building, according to our last names, which meant that I was separated from Michael and Stuart until the ceremony was over but had a clear view of Tracey throughout the night.

I was positioned between Cliff Townsend and Karen Turnbull. Cliff would appear on the list of the deceased. He would be killed in 2007, crushed to death when the jacks on his RV collapsed while he was underneath. He would be married with two sons and run a custom furniture business in Coquitlam. He seemed like a really nice guy.

Tracey stood directly across from me in the room we were in, about ten feet away me. She was between Sandra

Simms and Jeff Spadea. Before we left the room, I walked over to her and toyed incessantly with the tassel on her mortarboard, until I was forced to return to my line.

I had a diagonal view of Tracey in the theater from where I was seated, like the first time I saw her in English Lit. On our first graduation night, I stared at the back of her head and the left side of her face until she left her seat and walked down the nearest aisle to the stage, which was the last time I saw her before the prom.

☙❧

As we marched through the corridor between the waiting room and the theater, I saw Dad and Mom on my right, against the wall, surrounded by the other parents, and I saw Brad. His face was neatly shaved, his hair had been trimmed, and he was wearing a light olive green suit. He nudged my cap and pinched my collar as I went by.

When we took our seats inside the theater, and the novelty of our momentary celebrity began to ebb slightly, my eyes adjusted themselves, again, to a scarlet ray of light that reflected off of the stage. It partnered with the skulking shadows around the edges of the theater, which produced a crimson haze that hung over our heads.

Then I looked to the right, to the end of the row in front of me, where Tracey was seated. I held my gaze on her back until she turned and smiled in my direction.

ⱷ⋄ⱷ⋄

Fred Johnson was reelected valedictorian of our class. Again, he won by a landslide victory over the more obvious, and overqualified, candidates, all of whom lobbied much too hard for the position.

Again, we thought that selecting the school clown would somehow set our class apart from the rest.

Fred managed to strike a perfect balance between humor and sober reflection with his speech, which was titled "Our Place in the World." He drew the most laughter with the term "Nerds with Power," which he directed toward the handful of teachers who were in attendance that night.

The aisle on my right, where I stood after I left my seat, led to the bottom of a narrow staircase beside the stage, to the left of the podium. After the principal gave us our diplomas, we moved offstage, down into a well, and stood on a small piece of tape for the cap-and-gown picture.

The guys and I collected our cap-and-gown glossies in the school office the following week, on our way to seeing *Terminator 2*: *Judgment Day* at Eagle Ridge Cinemas.

When we entered the school office, it was obvious, from the thickness of the stack on the front counter, we were among the first to arrive, if not the first. When I saw that, I knew there was a good chance I would find Tracey's glossy before she ever got to see it.

I looked stiff and upright in my picture. The cap hovered on top of my oversized skull, and the picture show-cased my uneven nostrils much more honestly than any mirror had.

With the secretary scarcely looking in my direction but my friends anxious to leave, I rifled through the rest of the pictures, looking for Tracey.

After isolating the location of Tracey's glossy in the pile, I rearranged the pile on the counter so her picture was directly underneath mine. Then I pressed them together as if they were one. Banishing the guilt, which attacked me soon after I returned home, and the thought of Tracey's disappointment when she found her picture missing, I calmly slipped the picture into my pocket.

☙❧

"Tracey Simpson."

I'd already left my seat and was standing in the aisle with the rest of the grads in my line when Tracey floated across the stage in a single tranquil motion and collected her diploma. Her feet barely touched the floor. It took her eight seconds to move from one end of the stage to the other, and then she disappeared into the well, out of my sight.

My left foot was on the bottom of the staircase when I looked up and saw Cliff Townsend collect his diploma and then depart the stage and my thoughts.

"Ryan Tremblay," I heard the principal say.

Then all of the activity in the theater ceased, except for the tapping of my dress shoes. The principal was gone when I walked across the stage to collect my diploma, which was resting on top of the podium.

I didn't remember where we went, the first time, after we received our diplomas and had our cap-and-gown pictures taken, whether we returned to our seats or headed for the reception area. But when I looked out from the stage, the rest of the grads had their diplomas and were seated.

The gallery was dark.

"Ryan Tremblay," I thought I heard Tracey whisper in my ear.

The grads gave me a standing ovation, and then they all evaporated, except for Tracey. She was clutching her diploma, her eyes wide open, staring ahead.

I left the stage and ran toward her. When I waved my right hand across her face, standing in front of her, there was no response. I closed her eyes and kissed her forehead.

Then I looked up at the gallery. I saw my parents, Brad, Michael and Stuart, and the rest of the grads, who were out of their gowns. Everyone was dressed formally. They were older.

I saw Tracey Coreau and her husband.

I reached for Tracey's diploma.

The diplomas they gave us were printed on the cheapest parchment paper. But Tracey's was different that night. When I pulled it out of her grip, and slowly uncurled it, I felt the stark difference in the level of depth and hardness.

It was the premium heavyweight ivory paper that my fingers rubbed against. I barely flinched at the sight of the raised gold seal above the carefully inscribed letters of Tracey's name.

It was her master's degree.

৶৶৶

The small boxy room within the theater's reception area had no need for its lone window, a glass mailbox that stretched across the top of the opposite wall. Its narrow view—cars moving up and down a hill—was as useless as the tacky cheese straightening device on the snack table.

Before Tracey entered my life, the cheese straightening device and the pre-programmed traffic were the only visuals I'd retained from that part of the night. I immediately felt smothered, not by the claustrophobic setting but by my age, which had finally caught up with me.

When I looked out the window, I noticed that the traffic consisted of the same nine or ten cars, going in opposite directions. I saw my Honda Civic, and Dad's BMW, and Michael's Mustang. I turned to face the rest of the room, sensing that everyone was there for me, waiting for me to do or say something. They were pretending to have normal conversations around me, all for effect. It was all gibberish.

When I found myself standing next to Michael and

Stuart, I had no idea how I got there. I was afraid to even blink. The configuration of the room seemed to change every time I opened then closed my eyes. One moment my parents were on one side of the room, toward the door, and then they were circling the snack table.

I turned to Michael, who was closest to me. He was wearing a maroon jacket underneath his gown. My left hand brushed against his jacket. When I pulled my hand away, there were tiny drops of brown and red paint on my fingertips, which turned to dust when I rubbed my fingers together.

"It's all over," Michael said.

"Free at last," Stuart added.

"We'll always be friends," I said. "When we go our separate ways, get old and gray, turn into strangers, move far away and forget all of this, we'll still be friends."

Michael nodded. "We'll never lose touch. Our kids will play together, and our wives will be best friends."

"That's what I want," I said. "That's my dream for us."

"We'll never go away," Stuart promised me. "You'll never get rid of us."

I turned and saw Tracey on the other side of the room, no more than fifteen feet away, with her parents, taking pictures. She was wearing a beaded, sterling necklace, and there was a gold ring on her left hand. The middle fingers on her right hand were curled around the diploma, her high school diploma, which she held as if it were a badly printed theater program from a show that opened and closed on the same night.

She left her parents and walked over to me. We kissed, and then I steered her over to my parents. "This is Tracey," I said, putting my right arm around Tracey, maneuvering her until she was standing in between my parents for a picture. I took the camera from Mom. "Tracey and I have already met, Ryan," Mom reminded me as she looked at Tracey. "You look beautiful, Tracey."

"I saw your picture in the yearbook," Dad said to Tracey. "I wish Ryan had brought you over to the house for dinner."

"I'm glad that we're finally all together," Tracey said, pressing her cap against her chest as I steadied the camera.

I took one picture of Tracey with my parents, and then a second picture of them with Brad. Then Mom took the picture of me and Tracey, which I brought back with me to 2015.

It was the only picture I had of the two of us together.

Chapter 22

Although I stayed home on the day of the second prom, I talked to Michael, Stuart, and Tracey on the phone throughout the morning and afternoon. Brad was home with me, barricaded inside his room for most of the day, contemplating his future.

He knocked on the door as I was getting dressed then stood beside me in front of my bedroom mirror. "You're looking good," he said. "Have fun tonight, and tomorrow."

I was home the evening of Brad's prom in 1988, a rare Friday night apart from Michael and Stuart. I was upstairs, in my room, when I heard Brad leave the house. When I awoke the next morning, he still hadn't returned. I was out with Michael and Stuart when Brad barreled through the front door late on Saturday afternoon. He slept through Sunday.

"Do you remember your prom?" I asked him.

"I went with Debbie Olson," Brad recalled. "We had a great time."

Brad brought several girls home and into his room during his time at Moody Senior. I knew this because I heard each of the girls, who all made different noises. But Debbie was Brad's only steady girlfriend. She was the only girl Brad brought home for dinner, and her bookish glasses, curly blonde hair, and shyness instantly won over our parents. Her gentle speaking voice was very incompatible with the deep, guttural grunts Brad orchestrated from her body when he had her in his room, when Dad and Mom were out, when he knew I was home.

Debbie joined Brad at UBC after they graduated from Moody, but by the first Christmas break, she'd disappeared from the house, and Brad scarcely mentioned her afterward.

"Did you ever see her again?" I asked him.

Brad looked toward his room and nodded weakly. "I would see her around the campus after we broke up," he said. "She's really changed. I guess she'll be graduating next year."

I saw, in the bedroom mirror, Brad pause in the doorway on his way out of my room, watching over me. When I turned to look at him, he was already downstairs. I heard him open and close the refrigerator. Then he joined Dad and Mom in the living room. Dad and Mom had both left work early. Mom picked up my tuxedo on her way home.

❦

We sold the house in January 2016, or Brad did, less than two months after it was listed. We didn't argue over any of the details. The process ran smoothly, and Brad got a bit choked up when he planted the For Sale sign in front of the house.

After it was listed, during the ensuing weeks, as offers poured in and a sale looked imminent, I interspersed one of our business discussions with the announcement that Allison and I were getting married.

He congratulated me and was my best man at the wedding, which was held in the backyard of Allison's parents' house in April 2016, right around my forty-third birthday. I'd insisted on such a contained ceremony, embarrassed about my severe lack of family and friends.

I maintained sporadic contact with Brad afterward. There were Christmas cards, phone conversations, the occasional dinner, and he visited the hospital when my son was born.

On December 15, 2017, Brad was driving through the municipality of Hope with his wife and children when his SUV was struck by a semi-trailer truck on the Coquihalla Highway. The truck had skidded out of its lane, and this triggered a chain reaction on that stretch of the highway, which the newspapers described as being a virtual ice rink that day, following several days of freezing rain.

A florist van, which was carrying hydroponic equipment and multiple firearms, slammed into the SUV's fuel tank after the SUV flipped onto its side. The florist business was a front for a grow-op in the area, and the driver, not wanting any entanglements, panicked and was trying to dart around the pile up when he made solid contact with the SUV's fuel tank, which immediately erupted into flames. The driver ran away from the scene and was never found.

According to the witnesses at the scene, some of whom recorded the aftermath on their phones, Brad, his wife, and their two sons, who were on their way to the Big White ski resort in Kelowna, weren't killed instantly. It was highly likely that none of them lost consciousness before the inside of the SUV turned into a raging inferno, before the fire washed over them and ripped the flesh from their bodies. This made me squirm.

Brad's charred corpse instantly crumbled when the emergency workers tried to separate him from the seat he'd become one with. Although I took some comfort in the fact that we'd ended our relationship on genial terms, I was unable to expunge from my mind the image of my brother's inhumanly white eyeballs and teeth rattling around in a glass jar.

I placed Brad's obituary in the *Province*, the *Sun*, and, of course, the *Tri-City News*. I ended his obituary with the closing lines from the Robert Browning poem "Prospice," which was how I'd ended Dad's obituary and Dad ended Mom's.

☙❧

After I arrived downstairs in my prom tuxedo for the second time in my life in June 1991, I entered the living room, where I saw a baseball game on television. The Seattle Mariners, my favorite team, were playing the Toronto Blue Jays. On the first prom night, the Mariners defeated the Blue Jays by a score of three to one.

Brad was gone from the living room and the house. Dad and Mom were waiting for me in the living room. They locked hands and moved toward me. They surrounded me, as if they were holding an intervention. "Don't worry about us," Mom said. "Get on with your life."

Dad nodded in agreement to those words.

When the doorbell rang, I was looking at myself in the living room mirror, standing underneath the mantel, listening to Mom open the front door and welcome Michael and Stuart inside. Dad was beside me, on my right.

I turned and faced him. I lowered my hands to my sides as I stared down at him. Then I turned away from him and stepped into the hallway, joining Mom and Michael and Stuart, who watched impassively as Mom touched my face. With her left hand, she traced her fingers along the lines under my eyes and then lightly stroked my hair.

"Mom," I whispered.

Then she joined Dad in the living room, in death.

I turned to Michael and Stuart. Michael pulled on my left arm, and Stuart opened the door.

"Let's go," Michael said.

I took one last look into the living room and around the vacant house, and then my thoughts returned to Tracey. Following Michael and Stuart out the door, I saw the waiting limousine parked at the curb, facing uphill.

I locked the front door.

⟡⟡⟡

When I photographed high school grads, I noticed that the prom tuxedo had entered a time warp. The classic 1970s prom tuxedo—with the cufflinks, the disco shoes, the frills, and the accented ruffled shirt—was, as recently as 2015, enjoying a massive resurgence in popularity. By comparison, the Michael Jordan tuxedos—with the one button jacket, purple polyester liner, satin shawl lapel—seemed contemporary.

The prom dress allowed much more room for innovation, with endless permutations of colors, fabrics, hemlines, and necklines upon cocktail dresses, gowns, halters, skirts. Tracey's red dress had an ankle-length hem, and it was a dress—not any kind of ball gown she had to pull up with her as she walked. Of that much, I was sure.

The red dress sacrificed most of her legs, which was no small sacrifice, but was otherwise well-matched to Tracey's features. It accentuated her cheekbones and doe eyes, and it clasped her waist.

Besides the limousine that arrived in front of Tracey's house, the only other sign that something extraordinary was taking place in the cul-de-sac that evening was the appearance of a bronze Cadillac in Tracey's driveway. It had California plates and San Diego decals.

Tracey's father was very cordial toward me when he opened the front door and let me inside. But the politeness he extended to me inside the house that evening had a temporary feel and sound to it, as if he was certain that I would play no role in his, or his daughter's, future. He might've felt the same way about Anmore and Port Moody.

Tracey's parents sold the Anmore house in 1992 and moved to West Vancouver. Tracey's father died on February 16, 2015.

Feeling guilty about the advantage I had over Tracey's father, knowing how and when he was going to die, I stared straight ahead, toward the living room.

Tracey's brother, Todd, flashed in front of the living room entrance. He made ephemeral eye contact with me as he reached for what looked to be the *TV Guide* on a table. I didn't know what happened to him.

Then a man and woman, who were too young to have been Tracey's grandparents but had aunt and uncle written all over them, walked out of the kitchen. They grinned in my general direction as they headed to the living room.

When I heard the first serious commotion from upstairs, I focused on the bottom of the stairwell and then the wall that blocked my view upstairs. Then Tracey's mother arrived downstairs, wearing slippers, trailed by Tracey. Tracey's mother looked me over, twice, and then she stepped aside. Then I saw Tracey.

Blue—it was a blue dress. It was Maya blue. The back had been laced up, and the dress, which was made out of organza fabric, had been embellished with cascading ruffles and diamonds. The hemline was a-symmetrical, so the hem whirled around the back—and the sides—of her legs, and it shifted as she moved around. Her legs were plainly visible.

The dress featured a mermaid silhouette, and Tracey was wearing white gloves that covered her forearms. Her hair was cut to medium-length and was tilted slightly up-ward, which underscored the sterling earrings that jiggled slightly from her earlobes. She'd painted her lips with ruby lipstick, which was the only part of her that reminded me of the first prom night, and Chad Fletcher, who wasn't at the prom. He'd also disappeared from the class picture and the yearbooks.

Tracey's parents moved out of the hallway, to the edge of the living room entrance, where they watched me.

"I thought it was red!" I blurted.

"We were going to go with a red dress," Tracey said, "but we decided to go with blue. Do you like it?"

"It looks amazing," I said, stepping away from her in order to assimilate her luminescence, stopping at the edge of the doormat.

There was a honk from outside, which startled Tracey and me. A second honk followed a few seconds later, longer and louder. "It's time to go," I said, reaching out for Tracey, looking over at her parents, who hadn't moved.

I was momentarily locked in a staring contest with Tracey's parents, with Tracey caught in the middle. She looked puzzled at first, her eyes moving from side to side, as if she was watching a tennis match. I waited for her parents to turn away from us before I touched the door.

⌘

After leaving Anmore, we picked up Michael's prom date, Nicole Hunter, and then Stuart's prom date, Joanne McDougall, and then we headed for the Barnet Highway. When the girls started talking, it was obvious that Tracey hadn't had any prior contact with Joanne and Nicole, both of whom were members of the girls' basketball team.

"What about Robin and Shannon?" I asked Tracey, ready to tell the driver to stop and turn around. "Should we pick them up?"

"There's no need," she assured me.

"They're your best friends."

"They'll be fine without me," she said.

Michael and Nicole started kissing in the limousine, much more heavily than the first time I'd seen them kiss, which was in an upstairs hallway at school in the last semester, before the start of a class. Michael's back was against a wall when she leaned into him. It was only a peck, which was more sexual contact than I experienced throughout my twenties and thirties.

Our driver, Randy, had dirty-blond hair, which he let fall past his rippling shoulders, and his arm and shoulder muscles bulged every time he squeezed the wheel or made a turn. He was twenty-five, and he told us that he'd been driving the limousine for three years and wanted to open his own limousine service someday.

"Do you remember your prom?" I asked him.

"Of course," he said. "It was a great night. I was with my girlfriend, and my friends, just like you, although we didn't have a limo. We took my van."

"Do you keep in touch with them?" I asked.

He went still for a moment. Then he looked out the window and shook his head. "Actually," he said, turning to look at us, "I saw my old girlfriend a couple of years ago, when I picked her up at the airport. Can you believe that? I went to meet her, and we looked at each other, and I didn't recognize her at first, and then she said, 'Randy!' Whoa. I wasn't ready for that. She was so different—her body, her face, and especially her voice, which sounded American. She lives in Los Angeles. She's a publicist in Hollywood, and she was here for a movie she was working on. We talked on the way to the hotel, and when we arrived at the hotel and stepped out of the limo, she turned to me and said,

'No one will ever know me and see me the way you did.'
That was it."

He had the radio on LG73, the longtime top forty giant
that Zed toppled in a matter of weeks in the spring of 1991.
LG switched to a talk format in 1992, which didn't work.
"You'll remember the songs," he said, pointing at the radio
as Billy Idol's "Eyes without a Face" was playing. "That
was one of the songs we danced to, me and Bobbi, my girlfriend. Whenever I hear any of those songs, no matter where
I am, whoa, it's like a knife in the gut."

The limousine arrived at the Plaza of Nations at twenty
minutes to six, one of only two limousines I saw outside.
Randy parked on the waterfront walkway, between the
streets and the flags that flew overhead. "I'll be around here
the whole night," he assured us, pointing at the long line of
taxis waiting alongside the water. "Don't think about time,"
he urged us. "Pretend it's your last night on earth."

All of the plaza's glass structures, which were built for
Expo '86, would be gone by 2015, except for the one in
which our prom was held, which looked like a giant green-
house. It would become Edgewater Casino. The glass and
the walkway were all that would remain from our prom
night.

We joined the rest of the grads on the red brick walkway outside the building, waiting for Mr. Rockwell, the
prom chaperone, to open the glass doors. It was June 28,
1991, and we were all eighteen years old.

e/3e/3

When the music started to play, at seven, I led Tracey over to the middle of the slightly raised dance floor for the first song, which was Modern English's "I Melt with You."

Caroline Sherman and Trevor Wheeler were the first couple who joined us on the dance floor. I'd first seen them together at Banting, where Caroline, who always wore outdated dresses and thick-rimmed glasses, belonged to the academic elite, while Trevor, who was fifteen inches taller than her, was a *D&D* enthusiast. That was how my brother and I got to know him.

In 1987, when Brad was still at Moody Senior, Trevor visited our house several times. But Trevor, who thought of himself as a Dungeon Master but didn't care to follow most of the rules that were clearly specified in the *Dungeon Master's Guide* and the *Player's Handbook*, eventually entered into conflict with Brad, who ultimately expelled him from our basement for cheating.

Tracey and I kissed during the first slow song, which was Phil Collins's "One More Night." Our kisses on the dance floor were gentle and soft, our lips barely touching, which was the way I always saw myself greeting Tracey every morning when she was still in bed and very groggy. I was either saying goodbye or waking her up, while my fingers loosened the flakes from her eyelids and lashes.

By nine, the warm evening sun had receded into the

dim shadows at the bottom of the glass panels, which con-stricted space inside the building. Suddenly, the dance floor became packed, and the crowd of at least 200 followers filled the area between the front edge of the stage and the first row of chairs and tables. This left everyone else on an island and turned the rest of the plaza into a no man's land.

Tracey and I were outside, on the balcony, when I heard the opening of Madonna's "Crazy for you," which trans-ported me back to the first prom, to that piece of island in the middle of the plaza, far behind the dance floor and front tables. That's where I stood for most of the first prom night.

Then Tracey appeared. She'd emerged from the wash-room, on my left, no more than ten feet away from me. As we looked at each other, I felt the coat of armor slowly slip-ping off my shoulders as I moved toward Tracey, who didn't move or turn away.

I was less than five feet away from her, about to make the final lunge, when his chunky arms enveloped her. Then he guided her, without a hint of protest, onto the dance floor, where they kissed.

When my thoughts returned to my second prom night, I was standing behind Tracey out on the balcony. As the song finished, we were both looking out over False Creek, the body of water that separated the downtown core from the rest of Vancouver. My arms were around her waist, which was easily the most frequent pose I'd seen from all of the couples I'd photographed.

"This is our last night together," I said.

"We're still going to see each other," she insisted.

I broke free of her, only a few inches, standing in front of her, looking down into her eyes. Tracey then reached out and pulled me back into her.

"I'm trying to let go of you," I said. "I wish everything could stay like this forever, these past few weeks, but I know that would be a nightmare."

I took out my phone and showed her a picture of herself, and then one of her with Eric and the girls. "This is your life now," I said. "You have a family, and they need you. You belong to them now."

"Where'd you get that?" she asked, pointing at the phone.

"I live in the year 2015," I said. "So do you. We're both forty-two years old."

"Where did you get those pictures?"

"They're from your life," I said. "Look at them."

Before I could scroll through the rest of the images, she ripped the phone away from me and tossed it into the water. "I'm right here," she said.

"You don't know me," I said. "Not now, not ever."

❧❦❧

The sky was purplish with widening black splotches when Tracey and I rejoined the prom. Depeche Mode's

"Enjoy the Silence" was playing when we reentered the plaza. I briefly separated from Tracey during the song and approached the DJ. I reached into my pocket for an unlabeled tape, which I handed to him. I asked him to play the song "Under the Milky Way," the Church's astral, moody ballad of loneliness and romantic obsession. He agreed to play the tape after "Enjoy the Silence" ended.

The tape was entirely necessary, as was the twenty-dollar note I'd attached to it. Although "Under the Milky Way" made the top forty in 1988, the audience for alternative music was pretty much limited, between the late eighties and the beginning of the nineties, to freaks and weirdoes. I assumed that most of them didn't believe in proms.

But besides Chad Fletcher, I didn't notice anyone missing from the second prom, including Yuri Semenuk, who was with Helga Makkela. After "Enjoy the Silence" ended, I saw them leave the building together.

As I'd hoped, the opening lines of "Under the Milky Way" triggered an exodus. Tracey and I were alone on the dance floor. Her head burned into my chest as we moved in circles. When she looked up at me, I could see that she saw someone different. "You still look so good," she said, wrapping her arms around my neck. "You look so much younger than the rest of us."

Her right hand reached for my face until the fingertips settled against my curves and pores. As we rotated, I saw my reflection in one of the glass panels, which revealed the dark circles under my eyes and the hardening of my features. I was forty-two years old.

I looked over at the DJ's booth, which was empty. When "Under the Milky Way," rolled over to Jane's Addiction's "Jane Says," the nearly five minute song was allowed to play through. It was followed by the Chameleons' "Swamp Thing," which was the last song I heard that night.

"Did you like the songs I picked?" I asked Tracey. "I did the best I could."

"Perfect," she said.

I led Tracey off the dance floor and toward the glass doors we'd entered through in the early evening. I paused briefly at our table and touched Tracey's seat, which was cold. "Everyone's gone," I said, pointing at the tables, which were all empty. I watched pooling shadows consolidate into a black mass around the stage. "We have to leave."

Tracey Coreau nodded.

☙❧

Tracey and I took a taxi to the Bayshore, which was the preeminent hotel in Vancouver in 1991. It would only be a four-star hotel in 2015, indistinguishable from the rest.

The suite Dad booked for me overlooked Stanley Park—where I left my friends after the first prom—and a bay, which was redeveloped into Coal Harbor, an upscale condominium district and waterfront community, one of the most expensive neighborhoods in North America.

I was standing just inside the doors of the French balcony, staring out at the bay, monitoring the activity on the water, when I heard Tracey walk out of the bathroom. We were both naked. Her dress and my tuxedo were nowhere in sight.

She lay flat on her back on the bed. Then she pushed the covers away, revealing a thin layer of fat around her midsection, which I hadn't seen when we'd made love.

She pushed herself halfway upright on the bed. Then she reached for me.

When I took a step toward the front of the bed, I immediately felt myself being pulled in two different directions.

I was back in College Park, in my bedroom. My suitcase was packed, and I was staring into the yearbook drawer for the last time.

Chapter 23

When I awoke on April 7, 2018, the day I turned forty-five, I felt as if I'd lived more in the previous three years than the first forty-two combined. Between forty-two and forty-five, I'd fulfilled most of the requirements for adulthood and was dwelling less and less on the road not chosen. I tried exceptionally hard to focus solely on the life in front of me and my responsibilities to it.

Selling the house didn't sever my emotional ties to Port Moody, but it took away all of the reasons for being there. If I would have returned to Port Moody—College Park, the school—it would've been purely to indulge my fascination with loss. But I was becoming increasingly forgetful in my middle age, which wasn't a bad thing, certainly not for me.

After Allison and I were married, we bought a house in Surrey, a city in Metro Vancouver, right next door to Langley. The house was paid for with my share of Dad's estate.

In May 2018, about six months ago, Brad's estate was finally settled. This allowed Allison and me to sell the house in Surrey, which was known as the murder capital of Canada, and move into a much larger, nicer house in North Vancouver. The house had an oversized garage and a spacious backyard with a playground and a swimming pool. I learned to swim.

Money worries were non-existent, disarmingly so. From Dad's estate, I received more than two million dollars. In June 2018, one month before Allison and I bought the new house, I received the bulk of Brad's estate, which was valued at over four million dollars. My name didn't appear once in my brother's detailed, lengthy will.

Although I didn't ask for my brother's money, I didn't back away either. I hired a lawyer—a rather duplicitous, unsavory individual, who guided me through the ghoulish process, which he took joy in doing. The lawyers, mine and Brad's executor, prolonged the process as long as they could, which was how lawyers took care of each other.

I was the last of my family. I had no other living relatives, which left only my sister-in-law's family, who were scattered across the Southwestern United States. They happily accepted the paltry sum my lawyer offered them, at my urging, which was, in the grand scheme of things, a parking ticket.

I took everything. I sold Brad's house, without a real estate agent, and then, at my financial planner's urging, I liquidated the rest of his assets. Besides Brad's real estate holdings, he'd been heavily invested in gold and silver, whose prices were much too volatile for my liking. When everything my brother touched in his life—including all of the *Dungeons & Dragons* paraphernalia, which I gave to the liquidator—was gone, his image faded quickly. Then it was as if he'd never existed at all.

I felt that my brother and father would've approved of the decisions I made with their money, especially when I decided to get my nose and teeth fixed.

For my teeth, I went to one of those cosmetic dental studios with beverage service and plasma screens in the waiting area. The dentist barely flinched when he looked into my mouth for the first time but was unable to stop blinking. After poking at my teeth for a few minutes, he recorded each tooth, according to the level of decay, and assigned a score to each one. Then he took an X-ray.

I was expecting the worst, so when he finally gave me his assessment, anything short of having to wear dentures for the rest of my life would've been a relief.

"I can help you," he said as I looked up at him through the cloud of cotton he'd stuffed into my cheeks and jaw, "but it's going to be a long, painful process."

It took me nearly six months to complete all of the treatments, which included seven extractions and three root canals. The painkillers I was given barely made a dent in the nausea and pain. There were many nights when I howled like a werewolf, shaking and writhing in bed, and everywhere else in the house, my face puffed up to the size of a watermelon.

The extractions and root canals were followed by implants, which caused Allison to nickname me Jaws. After the dentist whitened my teeth, I had to get used to my new mouth, which changed slightly, from month to month, as it settled in. I had to relearn how to bite and chew. Then I had to learn how to smile.

The surgery to re-align my septum only took a few hours and was virtually painless. I took advantage of the opportunity to ask the plastic surgeon if he could give me an upgrade, which he did. I had a beautiful nose. My nose hairs were forced to go into hiding.

My enviable financial situation made me more, not less, determined to find a career that would consume the energy and time that would've otherwise been devoted to Tracey. Fatherhood and marriage failed to accomplish this. I had to move around constantly, because whenever I stopped, even for a second, she appeared.

After I quit photography, following the wedding at the golf club, I thought Allison might want to take over the studio in Langley or open her own photography business. But she also lost interest in photography, right around the time she became pregnant. She completed a one-year program at a tourism college in Vancouver, which helped her find a job at a visitor center in Vancouver. She told me she wanted to open her own tourism business, which I promised to finance.

By the fall of 2016, when I began searching for a meaningful career, I'd been away from post-secondary education for more than twenty years. I was approaching my mid-forties, so there was no point in going to SFU or UBC for a traditional degree. That would've been like remaining in high school after all of my contemporaries had graduated and left me behind. That was the story of one of my nightmares.

If photography had taught me anything, it was that I possessed some artistic flair and creativity, and this led me to apply to Vancouver Film School. I brought my photography portfolio with me on my first visit to the school, which occupied the top floor of a downtown Vancouver building, in the mistaken belief that I needed to impress them.

Their admission requirements were as simple as those of Douglas College. I was asked if I'd graduated from high school, and then someone checked my pulse. When I met with an advisor, it quickly became obvious that she was solely interested in how and when I would pay the hefty tuition.

I knew that the filmmaking program, which was my first choice, wasn't a practical starting point for someone

my age, so I instead chose animation. I'd always been in-
trigued by animation, and I had passable drawing skills,
which improved dramatically over the following year,
though I was never as good as Brad was. This would've
been perfect for him.

After taking a foundational course, which was manda-
tory, I paid $40,000 and enrolled in the one-year program.
The program consisted of twelve to fifteen hour days
throughout the year and encompassed all of the aspects of
compositing, drawing, lighting, modeling, surfacing, and
visual effects. I was exhausted all the time, which was com-
pounded by having a baby at home. I'd never been happier.

By the end of the program, I'd assembled an animation
reel, which the instructors were impressed enough with to
pass around to their network of contacts. This past February, about nine months ago, I was hired by a Vancouver animation studio as a production assistant. I looked at this as
my first real job.

The studio was very active in the production of week-
day morning cartoons and non-theatrical—if there was still
such a thing as a home video market, they would've been
classified as straight-to-video—films, including some Dis-
ney titles. As a production assistant, I assisted with special
effects, storyboarding, anything that needed to be done.

Everyone at the studio seemed to like me, and the feeling was mutual. I thought that my apprenticeship would last
two or three years, and then maybe they'd let me oversee

projects. Eventually, I'd direct and write, and I'd teach animation in my spare time, as many of my colleagues did. I thought I'd become a mentor.

I had a pet project going in my spare time, which was an animated short film I expected to have completed by early 2019. My film took animated characters from my company's projects and placed them inside 1980s video games. By the fall of 2018, I'd logged close to 300 hours on the film, which had a projected running time of slightly over two minutes.

So I was an adult. I officially became a man on March 22, 2017, when Rhys Matthew Tremblay was born—my son.

I played with him every morning before I left the house and when I came home. Our father-son rituals, which included watching *Masters of the Universe* and *The Transformers* on the cartoon channel every Friday night, and *The Incredible Hulk* on Saturday nights, expanded daily throughout his first year. Before he reached his first birthday, I'd already slid a miniature hockey stick in between his tiny fingers. I wanted to get him—and myself—skating lessons as soon as possible. Then we'd try baseball, basketball, football, anything but soccer.

In August 2018, Allison became pregnant again. It was another boy, and we were, by November, still in the process of choosing a name for the baby, which was due in May 2019, just after my forty-sixth birthday.

Allison seemed to love me, and I'd learned to love her. I thought we were going to be okay. I was overjoyed with our son, and the one on the way, but I was secretly hoping for girls.

ↄ◦ↄ◦ↄ

Everything I'd done throughout the previous three years had been geared toward distracting me from thoughts of Tracey, but there were times when I was not very strong. That was when I got scared.

At forty-five, loving her was like being stranded on an alien shore that fell under a partial eclipse. I could see the ship made of her life blowing across the reddish, shadowy horizon, left to right and right to left. It always appeared close enough to touch but was in another realm. I maintained a signal fire, and I waved a flaming stick back and forth in front of my face, anything to attract its attention. But it had no destination, and I knew she'd never find me. I grasped this.

Last night, November 20, 2018, after I rubbed Allison's belly and then put Rhys, who was on the verge of switching from crib to bed, to sleep, I entered my office and locked the door.

The room contained an antique oak desk and leftover photographic equipment. The walls were covered with animation art. I set my laptop down on the desk but didn't open it that night. Some nights, when it was quiet, I just sat there and thought about Tracey.

I opened the window and waited for the cool November breeze to reach the closet before I plopped myself down in the task chair. I sighed, and then I turned my head to the right and looked down at the two locked drawers. Then I took out a key, which I spun in front of my eyes before I unlocked the bottom drawer. I removed the pictures of Tracey.

There was me and Tracey at the graduation ceremony.

There was Tracey with my parents.

There was Tracey, in the bikini, at Beach Bash.

I stared at the pictures until my eyes lost perspective, and then I put them back in the drawer. Then I slid the chair over to the closet, where I kept the yearbooks. Besides those pictures, the only other proof that existed of my second life in June 1991 was my newest copy of the 1991 yearbook. This was all that returned to 2015 with me, except for my memories.

The yearbooks were in the same box as my *Dummies* books and hardback graphic novels, not because I was hiding them but because that was where yearbooks belonged after more than twenty-seven years. I protected mine with bubble wrap.

Twenty-seven years. It only felt like it'd been that long when I said it out loud. Twenty-seven years. I didn't know where it'd gone.

It seemed like only yesterday we were together. When I measured the actual distance that existed in my mind between June 1991 and November 2018, and I included what happened to me in October 2015, it'd been just over three years since I'd last touched her.

My original copy of the 1991 yearbook literally fell apart and had to be thrown away. I kept the newer copy, the one with Tracey's signature inside, inside a plastic sleeve, with a backing board, as if it was the first issue of *Amazing Spider-Man*. The pages were white.

I slid back over to the desk, and the heart of the breeze, and then I opened the yearbook. I turned to the color picture and then to Tracey's headshot. When I touched her face, the years fell away.

I was eighteen again.

I was in the school office, watching the seniors walk to and from the back of the office, where the grade twelve headshots were taken.

I walked down the first corridor, and when I turned left and looked to the end of the next corridor, I saw Tracey standing in line, waiting to enter the curtain of the makeshift photo booth.

I was standing beside her, on her left, when a senior—it was Brian LaForge, whom I didn't know—appeared from behind the curtain. He handed Tracey the rancid gown we all shared for the picture. When she entered the booth, I stepped forward. I was almost standing over the Jostens photographer's shoulder when he snapped Tracey's head-shot.

I felt myself slouching in the chair. I heard the loud creak. Then I heard my son crying and my wife going to him.

When Tracey exited the photo booth, we were alone in the back of the office, standing between the long corridor, the photo booth, the offices, and a window. The window looked out on the front of the school, which was deserted and silent. The upper parking lot was empty except for my Honda Civic.

I was a mute spectator. My arms were pinned to my sides. I thought I was invisible to her even as she looked right at me. She offered me the gown, which fell to the floor.

Then she walked past me, out of the office. Her back was facing me until she reached the end of the narrowing corridor and stopped. Then the right side of her face turned slightly in my direction, just before she disappeared around the corner.

I closed the yearbook and went to bed.

About the Author

David Grove is an author, film journalist, and a produced screenwriter from Vancouver, Canada. A film historian, he's the author of the books *Fantastic Four: The Making of the Movie*, *Jamie Lee Curtis: Scream Queen*, *Jan-Michael Vincent: Edge of Greatness*, *Making Friday the 13th*, and *On Location in Blairstown: The Making of Friday the 13th*. *The Yearbook* is his first novel.